W9-AHL-692

A Great Idea!

We have selected some of the novels
of Harlequin's world-famous authors
and combined them in a 3-in-1 Omnibus series.

You get THREE enjoyable, full-length romances,
complete and unabridged,
by the same author,
in ONE deluxe, paperback volume,
every month.

A Great Value!

Almost 600 pages of pure entertainment
for an unbelievably low price,

ONLY $1.95.

A truly "Jumbo" read,
available wherever paperback books are sold.

FIRST VOLUME
ON SALE
FEBRUARY 1976

OTHER
Harlequin Romances
by REBECCA STRATTON

Many of these titles are available at your local bookseller,
or through the Harlequin Reader Service.

For a free catalogue listing all available Harlequin Romances,
send your name and address to:

HARLEQUIN READER SERVICE,
M.P.O. Box 707, Niagara Falls, N.Y. 14302
Canadian address: Stratford, Ontario, Canada N5A 6W4

or use coupon at back of books.

THE FIRE
AND THE FURY

by

REBECCA STRATTON

HARLEQUIN BOOKS   TORONTO
WINNIPEG

Original hard cover edition published in 1975
by Mills & Boon Limited

SBN 373-01942-4

Harlequin edition published January 1976

CHAPTER ONE

DORCAS stood quite still for a moment and let the almost chill tranquillity of the little church lie like a cooling hand on her hot forehead. A party of tourists who had just departed were still faintly audible ouside in the hot sunshine of the Plaza de San Julio, but inside the church it was cool and still and quite blessedly peaceful.

A somewhat plump white stone Virgin smiled down at her benevolently in the soft light from the many flickering candles arrayed at her feet by devout visitors, so that for a moment Dorcas found herself almost smiling in return. No devout pilgrim herself, she nevertheless appreciated the tranquil calm of the place and in the full heat of the day she felt she needed a moment to cool off.

It was not her first visit to the church by any means, for it held an irresistible fascination for her and she had got into the habit of coming in to see it whenever she drove into San Julio, usually with Rafael. The thought of Rafael brought another smile to her lips and this time she did not restrain it.

Rafael was one of the nicest things to happen to her since she came to Spain. She had met him first while she was out shopping and he had taken it upon himself to dismiss the taxi she had hired and drive her back to Casa de las Rosas himself. Since then they had met several times, though only once by accident, and Dorcas enjoyed his company more than anyone's—except Ramón's, of course.

Following her usual habit, she turned from the main aisle suddenly and walked down one of the shorter side aisles that ran across the width of the little church, quartering it into the shape of a cross. At the end of this aisle was another niche, edged by intricately worked stone and housing another holy statue which in turn had a garland of flickering candles at its feet, and she smiled at the familiarity of him.

San Julio, after whom the town, the *plaza* and the church were named, was a favourite of Dorcas's, and she often came to see him—in part to admire the artistry of the ancient carving, but also because she liked his calm, benign look, and the uncanny suggestion of patience in his blank stone eyes.

Her shoes made no more than a soft whisper of sound on the cool stone floor and for a while she heard no other in the quiet of the church until briefly, off to her right somewhere, a faint swish of movement betrayed another presence. Only momentarily startled by it, Dorcas paid little attention, thinking it was most likely a solitary penitent whispering his 'aves' in the cloistered silence.

Out of deference to tradition Dorcas had covered her head with a lacy scarf that enveloped her from the crown of her head to her shoulders and almost completely shrouded the thick, golden-fair hair that showed above lightly tanned features and below the edge of the lace scarf at the back.

The soft church lighting suggested a near-classic

6

perfection in the curve of her cheeks and the fluttering candlelight touched her blue eyes with a shadowy glow and her mouth with a hint of fullness. Being not very tall she was obliged to angle her head quite sharply when she looked up at San Julio in his niche, and the lacy scarf fell back from her face, showing two golden wings of hair on either side of it.

The benign features of the stone saint bore no resemblance at all to the only other Julio she knew of, and she pulled a rueful face when she recalled the man who was such a constant source of irritation to her. Don Julio Valdares owned the vast estate that adjoined her half-brother's much smaller property, and his main aim in life, so it seemed to Dorcas, was to acquire Ramón's land and attach it to his own—something that Ramón Lorenzo, her half-brother, was reluctant to do.

There was much about Spain that Dorcas liked, and she got on well with the few people she had met, but Don Julio Valdares was not one of them, and she had said many times in the privacy of her brother's home that she disliked him intensely. He was arrogant, callous and cruel, all these adjectives she used freely to describe their wealthy neighbour, and she had vowed many times to tell him so at the first opportunity. In fact the few times she had come within speaking distance of him she had found herself so annoyingly tongue-tied that she had allowed him to pass with no more than a very brief and formal greeting in Spanish.

Dorcas was fond of Ramón, and the fact that he was partially crippled made her almost fiercely protective towards him, despite the fact that he was fifteen years older than she was and well able to run his own affairs. He often laughed about Dorcas's air of protection, but she knew that he also enjoyed her affection and treated her more in the way of a favourite uncle than a half-brother.

Dorcas's mother had been married at eighteen to Paco Lorenzo whom she met while on a holiday in Spain, and they had enjoyed twelve happy years together before Paco died of pneumonia while on their first visit to England since their marriage. Mary Lorenzo, overcome by grief, did not return to Spain but stayed in England with her eleven-year-old son, and two years later married again.

Henry James was some years her senior and nearly sixty when their daughter, Dorcas, was born. Ramón, fifteen years old then and restless for the warmer climate of his native country, returned to Spain to live with an uncle and aunt, the same aunt who now shared his home and acted as his hostess, for he had never married.

Three years ago Henry James too had died and his widow was now contemplating marrying for a third time, and it was because of her dislike of her prospective stepfather that Dorcas was in Spain. She had celebrated her twenty-first birthday a little over three months before and her father had left her financially independent, so that there was no need for her to find work and she could more or less please herself where she went.

A rather tentative letter to Ramón suggesting a visit had brought an invitation to stay as long as she cared to and so far she had enjoyed every minute of her stay. The only cloud on the horizon was Ramón's bloodless battle with Don Julio Valdares to keep his land, and that need not really have concerned her as much as it did.

Determinedly dismissing the autocratic don from her thoughts, she glanced up again at the face of the saint and smiled. If only his namesake could have displayed as much benignity she would have been less inclined to dislike him. Stepping back, she turned swiftly, ready to face the hot Spanish sun again, and caught her breath when she almost collided with someone. Her eyes wide and startled, she put a hand to her throat and stared.

'Siento molestare, señorita!'

The voice was deep, quiet and masculine, and a man stepped from the shadows outside the flickering glow of the candles. For a moment Dorcas nearly believed him to be a figment of her imagination, he was so unexpected, but then she recognised him and surprise changed to discomfiture.

He was a tall, lean, towering figure in the dim coolness, a disturbingly secular and virile shape among the stone saints and the sacred tranquillity of the church, and it crossed her mind briefly to wonder what he was doing there. He had a strangely compelling air of arrogance about him too that registered oddly in such surroundings and the strong dark features were much too suggestive of earthy pride to bear any likeness to his name saint who looked down benignly on them both.

The heaving deck of a Moorish corsair would have made a more fitting background for him than the cool quiet of the little church, and his bearing suggested that he knew it well enough. A faint scar showed lighter on the deeply tanned neck, just below his jaw on the right-hand side, and another

9

across the back of his right hand.

Dorcas had noticed them vaguely before, but at close quarters they were much more apparent—not long thin scars such as a cut would leave, but drawn patches of lighter skin as if the flesh had been burned and was not yet healed sufficiently to blend with the dark tan of its surroundings. The scars, she felt, served only to add to the suggestion of piratical ruthlessness, and even in a church Don Julio Valdares seemed to dominate everything around him.

Dorcas shook her head a little dazedly, trying to gain control of her wildly racing heartbeat and quite illogically resenting the effect he had on her. She had seen him only with a distance of several yards between them before, and while he was mounted on one of the beautiful but highly strung horses he bred, and each time she had found him oddly disturbing. Now in the closer proximity of the silent church he seemed even more so.

He was taller than she expected, for one thing, and there was a steely arrogance about the way he held his powerful, lean body that, as a woman, she was bound to find attractive no matter what her opinion of him was. The fact that he also bred fighting bulls for the *corrida* was another point against him in Dorcas's eyes, for she abhorred the traditional sport of Spain and made no secret of it.

Suddenly aware that not only was she still gazing at him blankly but also that his gaze had lingered for rather a long time on the bright wings of her hair, she put up a hand to draw the lace scarf closer to her face, checking that her head was still covered.

'Señorita James?' he enquired softly, and Dorcas blinked in surprise. Not because he knew her name or that his English was so good, but because it was startling to come across a Spaniard of Don Julio's standing approaching a young woman without observing the proper formalities.

'I—I'm Dorcas James,' she admitted warily, and Julio Valdares inclined his head in the briefest of formal bows. A glimmer of expression in his dark eyes suggested that he recognised her dislike but refused to be deterred by it.

'We have not met formally, *señorita*,' he said. 'Allow me to introduce myself more fully. I am Julio Esteban de Valdares y Montevida.' The flowery Spanish introduction might have impressed Dorcas more if Ramón had not prepared her for it. As it was she merely followed his example and inclined her head slightly to acknowledge the introduction. 'You admire our church, *señorita*?' he asked.

'It's—it's very pretty,' Dorcas said, unable to find a more enthusiastic answer. It was maddening to find herself tongue-tied by his overpowering personality, yet again, and she resented it.

One brow elevated to the swathe of black hair that covered half his broad forehead. 'Pretty?' he echoed, and Dorcas wished she had chosen a less prosaic description.

'It's beautiful,' she amended, and momentarily a hint of smile touched the wide straight mouth, and he looked round the little church as he spoke.

'We think so, *señorita*,' he said. 'It is very old and has a great history.'

'Ramón told me.' She hastened to let him know

11

that she was not merely sightseeing, although he must know that she did not worship there if he did so himself. For a moment she hesitated, aware that he was watching her with a curious air of expectation, and she wondered if he knew just how tempted she was to say the things she had imagined so often saying to him.

But even had she had the nerve to open such a conversation, a church was not the place to indulge in personalities and she felt herself at a complete loss for words, wishing only to escape into the open air again, no matter how hot it was outside. She glanced at her wristwatch, without really seeing the time, and half-smiled as if in regret. 'If you will excuse me, Señor Valdares,' she said in a voice that sounded oddly hushed in the silent church, 'I have to go.'

'You are returning to the Casa de las Rosas?' he asked, and Dorcas hesitated, though heaven knew why, except that she had a suspicion at the back of her mind of what he was going to say.

'Yes, I am,' she admitted at last, and he inclined his head again, stiffly formal.

'If I might offer my services, Señorita James,' he said in that deep, quiet voice, 'I would be pleased to drive you.'

The offer took Dorcas completely by surprise and for a moment she simply stared at him. She had suspected he had the delivery of a message to Ramón in mind, but to offer to drive her home was the last thing she expected. She shook her head hastily, too hastily for politeness, as his frown showed.

'No, thank you, *señor*,' she said. 'A friend is

driving me!'

'Ah!' The dark eyes glittered in the soft lighting and lent an even harsher contrast to the surrounding peace and quiet. 'Señor Montez!'

Swiftly Dorcas looked up, her eyes uneasily suspicious, though for no really good reason. It was quite possible that he knew Rafael and possible too that he had seen them driving together, but it was no concern of his and she disliked the hint of disapproval she thought she detected in his voice.

The way she angled her chin and looked down her small nose at him was unconsciously haughty, but she meant to let him know that her affairs were nothing to do with him and she chose to ignore the invitation to deny or confirm that Rafael had driven her into town. 'If you will excuse me, *señor*,' she said in a small but cool voice, and waited for him to move out of her way.

'*Claro, señorita!*' His brief bow, Dorcas felt, was as much mocking as polite, and she slipped past him hastily, her footsteps clicking softly on the cool stone floor, anxious only to put as much distance as possible between them.

Prompted by heaven knew what instinct, she turned when she reached the central aisle and glanced back. He still stood beside the statue of his namesake, tall and arrogant and quite out of place in the quiet little church, his dark eyes watching her with a disturbing steadiness, glowingly jet black under the yellow light.

'*Hasta la vista, señorita!*' His voice, despite its softness, carried easily in the echoing silence of the church and Dorcas hastily turned again and hurried along the main aisle and out into the heat of

13

the *plaza*, letting the heavy door swing to behind her with a soft thud.

'Till we meet again' was a provocative thing for him to have said in the circumstances, but she supposed that further meetings with him were inevitable while she went on indulging in her favourite form of exercise. Walking was a less appropriate pastime in the heat of Spain, but she still enjoyed it, and the tree-lined boundary between her brother's land and Don Julio's offered a shady alternative to her native Surrey lanes.

She sometimes wished she had learned to ride, for it would certainly have been an advantage in the present circumstances, but she never had, any more than she had ever learned to drive a car. It would have been rather a boost to her confidence to be able to face Julio Valdares on his own level.

Hurrying across the *plaza* towards the fountain where she was to meet Rafael, she tried to banish Don Julio Valdares from her thoughts with an impatient shrug. Waving a hand to Rafael as she hurried the last few yards, she realised ruefully that a man like Don Julio would not be easy to dismiss, nor would those softly spoken words he had used in parting. They might almost have been taken for a challenge, she thought, and frowned over the idea.

Dorcas's bedroom at the Casa de las Rosas was a constant source of delight to her, for its view was breathtaking and quite different from anything she was used to in England. Initially, it was true, she had found a certain harshness in the hot Spanish countryside that contrasted strongly with the cooler, gentler leafiness of her native Surrey, but now that she was more accustomed to it she found it had a beauty of its own.

The harsh, arid sweep of the upper slopes of the hills gave rise to the life-giving water before it was channelled into a centuries-old irrigation system for the more lush lower slopes. It was a country that lacked any form of encouragement from nature to grow crops, but the dark-foliaged olive trees grew in orderly lines where the water supply flourished, and the occasional vineyard straggled along in paler contrast, defying the relentless sun to produce their crops.

A sliver of dusty road sheared its way across the brassy countryside and disappeared where it entered the suddenly fertile area close to where the little stone houses of the village sat squat and mellow in the heat. Higher up the hill, but even more lush, thanks to irrigation, stood Ramón's home, Casa de las Rosas, and only a quarter of a mile further on the much more ostentatious villa of Don Julio Valdares, Las Furias—The Furies.

From her bedroom window Dorcas could look out over quite a bit of Don Julio's vast estate. She could even catch a glimpse of the villa itself, a large white building that was almost completely hidden by the vegetation that surrounded it. Tall feathery palms and a profusion of other trees and shrubs clustered close about it as well as between its white walls where the inevitable *patio* would be.

A little further down the hill and closer to Ramón's land were the stables and the paddocks, sheltered from the full heat of the Spanish sun by enormous umbrella-shaped fig trees that allowed no more than an occasional glimpse of the shiny-coated horses that grazed there.

The whole estate was so huge and spread so far that it was not possible for her to see all of it, even from her vantage point, and once again she frowned over the greed of a man who was not content with so much but also wanted Ramón's much smaller property as well.

Not that Ramón's estate was small, except in comparison with his neighbour's, for it straggled down as far as the village at the very bottom of the hill, but in contrast to the average garden in England it was enormous. It too had once supported crops of olives and even a few vines, but over the years, since Ramón's accident, the trees and the land had become badly neglected and the crops were no longer commercially viable.

Badly injured in a riding accident six years before, Ramón had once been told he would never be able to even sit upright again, but he had proved them all wrong, although his interests now lay entirely in an export business that operated out of the port of Cádiz.

The production of crops from the fruit trees needed more personal attention than he was able to give since his accident, but the export business enabled him to be fully independent and work from his home. It was because the land was not being fully exploited that Don Julio wanted it, but Ramón was not anxious to lose what property he still possessed, and refused to sell, a decision that Dorcas supported wholeheartedly, although she suspected Ramón's aunt did not.

Doña Teresa was the widow of his father's brother, and she had looked after him since he returned to Spain at fifteen. She was a small, plump and gentle woman of about sixty, and she delighted in having Dorcas with them. Her own daughters were all married and lived too far away to visit very often and she treated Dorcas very much like one of her grandchildren. Her refusal to dislike Don Julio with the same implacable determination that Dorcas did herself was her one fault as far as Dorcas was concerned.

Leaning out of the arched window shaded by hanging vines of wisteria, Dorcas reached down and cupped a creamy-headed rose in one hand. The whole villa was draped in the heavy-scented profusion of climbing roses and gave it its name, but the sweet-scented, mauve wisteria was almost as profuse. Climbing its tortuous way from the garden below, it hung in great plumes of blossom beside, below and above her window, making the slatted shutters virtually inoperable.

The *patio* beyond the arched shelter of the balcony that supported the upper rooms was always so peaceful and cool and Dorcas never tired of it. She had never seen flowers grow in such quantities before, crowding each other in stone urns and cascading over the rim of the fountain's basin were geraniums, roses and carnations, while more roses and some magnificent magnolias vied with sheltering orange and lemon trees to provide a heady air of perfume for the paved *patio*.

The fountain, small by some standards, was the main feature of the arrangement and was not only visually pleasing but audibly too, its soft tinkling sound soothing amid the exotic colours and scents. On the far side a tall wrought-iron gate gave access from the private road, the inevitable palms that were such a feature of southern Spain, casting their feathery shade across half the area. It was comforting to think that, if she chose to, she could spend the rest of her life in such surroundings.

Suddenly made aware by her stomach's demands that it was almost time for dinner, she broke the cream rose from its branch and tucked it, with a dash of bravado, into her hair and behind her ear. Its petals were cool and soft against her skin and she turned and took a last look at herself in the long mirror before she went downstairs.

Even walking downstairs made her aware of the enormous difference between her half-brother's house and the one she had shared with her mother in England. Nothing here bore the slightest resemblance to the typical English home, but gave pleasure to the eye everywhere she looked.

Black wrought-iron balustrades, intricately curved, followed the line of a white marble staircase as it swept down into a wide, cool hall, tiled with the exquisite patterns of Moorish *azulejos*. The hall was small in length despite its width, but it had an exquitely eastern look that Dorcas loved and she never tired of admiring it.

The dining-room had always struck Dorcas as a direct contrast to the Moorish look of the hall, but it, in its way, was beautiful too. Long and wide, its ceiling dark-raftered, it had white walls and high arched windows decorated with Moorish stonework and shaded by the overhang of the balcony above it. Dark, heavy polished wood furniture gave it an air of grandeur and several small but valuable paintings hung on the walls, their colours muted by the shadowy light. It was a simple room in fact, but it had an air of richness that was impressive.

After a few initial upsets when she first arrived, Dorcas had taken to Spanish food and now thoroughly enjoyed it, although she always enquired into the antecedents of any new dish that was offered her. Both Ramón and his aunt were watching her now as she studied a plate of what appeared to be some kind of meat in gravy, and she knew Ramón was smiling to himself.

'What is wrong, *chiquita*?' he asked at last. 'What do you imagine Mercedes has served for us, hmm?'

Dorcas looked at him and screwed up her nose, her eyes sparkling with laughter for his good-natured teasing. 'I wish I knew,' she confessed. 'It smells delicious and it looks good too, but what is it?'

'*Riñones al Jerez*,' Doña Teresa informed her with a smile, and Ramón laughingly translated.

'Kidneys in sherry, Dorcas, you will enjoy them!'

'I'm sure I shall!' She started to eat, closing her eyes momentarily in delight over the flavour of the dish, and Ramón laughed.

'You do not dislike very much, I think,' he said, and it was evident he approved of her enthusiasm. 'It is good to see you eat so well, is it not, Tía Teresa?'

'*Muy bien!*' Doña Teresa agreed with a smile. 'And to stay so—so slender too!' She glanced at her own ample proportions and pulled a rueful face. 'I was never so slender!'

'You are what is called in England—cuddly, is that not right, Dorcas?' Ramón asked. 'And that is how most Spanish men would prefer you—we have a taste for the more voluptuous shape, no?'

He rolled his eyes expressively and laughed, and not for the first time Dorcas pondered on how very Spanish her half-brother was. It was difficult sometimes to realise that her own mother had also given birth to Ramón, who was as Spanish as he could be except for his lighter brown hair. His eyes were as dark as his father's must have been and he had that fine, strong bone structure that in some men suggested ruthlessness.

Doña Teresa's gentle eyes were looking at her with a hint of mischief in their depths and her mouth smiled as she spoke, though not in the least maliciously. 'Not all Spanish men, I think, Ramón,' she corrected him gently. 'I think Rafael Montez has a taste for slender women, hmm? With long golden hair and blue eyes?'

Ever ready to tease her, Ramón winked an eye and looked across at his sister. 'Ah, si, I forgot the dashing Señor Montez,' he said with pseudo-gravity. 'Of course he prefers slender fair women, as you say, Tía Teresa!'

Refusing to be embarrassed by their teasing, Dorcas got on with her meal, glancing only briefly at Ramón and wrinkling her nose. 'I bumped into Don Julio Valderes this afternoon while I was in San Julio,' she said, and Doña Teresa who was unfamiliar with the phrase in its English use, looked startled.

'How did such a thing happen?' she enquired. 'Did Señor Montez collide with his car?'

'Oh no, Tía Teresa.' Dorcas laughed, shaking her head over the misunderstanding, 'I mean that

I—I met him accidentally. I was standing in the church looking at his saintly namesake when he just appeared from somewhere in the church and nearly frightened me to death for a minute.'

Ramón, who had never actually expressed a dislike of the man who was so determinedly trying to dispossess him, looked at her curiously for a moment. 'Were you polite?' he asked then, and Dorcas pouted her dislike of the suggestion that she would be other than polite to a stranger, no matter how much she disliked and disapproved of him.

'Of course I was polite, Ramón,' she told him reproachfully. 'I'm not bad-mannered, I hope, but I was cool and left him in no doubt how I feel about him.'

'He is a very—interesting man,' Doña Teresa said, seeking the right word to convey her meaning, and Dorcas looked at her disapprovingly.

'He's a very arrogant and unlikeable one,' she decreed firmly, and did not miss the swift exchange of glances between Ramón and his aunt.

'You are possibly a little prejudiced, *pequeña*,' Ramón suggested gently, and Dorcas, unable to deny it, shrugged her shoulders.

'There's one thing about him that puzzled me,' she said after a moment or two. 'He has what look like scars on his neck and on his right hand. I've noticed them before, but today, at close quarters, they were even more evident. Are they burn scars?'

'They would be,' Ramón guessed. 'Nearly seven years ago there was a serious fire in the stables at Las Furias and some of the horses were lost. Valdares and his *caballerizo* managed to save most of them, but Valdares was burned quite seriously because he went in for a stallion who was trapped.'

'Oh! Oh, I see!'

Somehow the role of rescuer did not fit in with Dorcas's preconceived ideas of Don Julio Valdares, although if only she considered it seriously those strong features suggested as much courage as ruthlessness. But to think of him risking his neck and being seriously burned to rescue his animals gave her a completely new conception of the man, and one that made her oddly uneasy.

As long as she saw him only as a cold and ruthless persecutor of her crippled half-brother she could more easily ignore his attractions as a man, but with this new light on his character it might prove more difficult. She had no hesitation in admitting to herself that she found him attractive, even though he was Ramón's age or more, for Julio Valdares was the kind of man that any woman was attracted to.

'He is also a very *brave* man,' Doña Teresa suggested softly, breaking into her thoughts, and Dorcas, bound to admit it, nodded.

'I have to admire a man who takes such risks because he loves his animals,' she agreed.

Doña Teresa looked briefly puzzled. 'The horses were very valuable,' she told Dorcas in her soft voice. 'He could not afford to let them die.'

For a moment Dorcas felt a cold twist of horror at the sheer callous practicality of it, then she nodded, understanding at last. Fear for his profits fitted in far better with her picture of Don Julio than a love of the beautiful animals he bred, but she could not help feeling a sense of disappointment when she recognised it.

CHAPTER TWO

IT was always a pleasure to wake up in such a room, Dorcas thought sleepily, and smiled to herself as she stretched her arms wide. The scent of flowers from the *patio* below her window filled the room, carried by the cooler morning air, and she sniffed it appreciatively as she swung her feet out of bed and into her slippers.

It was bound to be a good day today because she was seeing Rafael, and that always made her happy. They were driving into San Julio for lunch and then going for a drive up into the hills. It was a plan that both Ramón and his aunt approved of, although sometimes Dorcas thought Doña Teresa worried a little about her spending so much time with Rafael unaccompanied.

On the whole her friendship with him was viewed with favour, but she wondered if Ramón would agree to a more serious relationship if such a thing became likely. She had known Rafael for a little over two months now and she was ready to admit that she found him very attractive, but so far she had avoided making any firm decision about how she really felt about him.

She sat for a moment on the edge of the big square bed, her fingers idly stroking the softness of hand-embroidered lace sheets, and thought about

Rafael. She knew very little about him if she was honest, and Ramón knew only that he was of a wealthy family from a district some five or six kilometres away. He was good-looking and charming and showed every sign of enjoying her company, but beyond that she had to confess to knowing nothing.

He had so far made no suggestion that their present lighthearted, flirtatious association should become anything more serious, and that, in some way, puzzled her, for despite the conventions binding the Spanish male to certain patterns of behaviour with his own countrywomen, they seldom showed such restraint with visiting English girls.

If Rafael was likely to become more seriously interested in her, of course, there would be all sorts of snags to overcome, but so far the question had not arisen. She preferred not to try and analyse her own feelings at the moment, and shrugged off the matter as she went to have her bath. Rafael, at the moment, was no more than a very pleasant companion for drives and the occasional lunch date, and nothing else need concern her until it happened.

It was usually during the cooler part of the day, in the hour or so after the customary late Spanish breakfast, that Dorcas took her daily walk, and today was no exception. She was not seeing Rafael until after two o'clock for their luncheon date, so there was plenty of time.

Dressed in a trim white dress that flattered her golden tan, she set off from the house. Dark glasses protected her eyes from the glare of the sun, while her arms and legs were bare to encourage her skin to tan even more deeply. Ramón had told her that she should have worn a hat to protect her head, but she had long since dispensed with such protection. Under the trees it was safe enough to go bare-headed.

The twisty, ghost-like shapes of the neglected olives spread their grey arms against the coppery blue sky, and looked a little sad somehow in their neglect, while along the boundary where she walked, plane and eucalyptus trees stretched their branches wide enough to make a shady walk for her. The gaunt, straggling shape of Ramón's land ran with undulating boundaries as far as the cluster of whitewashed, thatched *casetas* that made up the village, huddled beside the dusty streak of road.

Nothing was as idyllic as it looked, she knew that, but while she could keep her mind firmly on the outward appearance of things and not dwell on the poverty she knew existed in the primitive little *casetas*, there was a certain harsh beauty to be found that attracted her. It was, she realised with a start, the same kind of contradiction that made Don Julio Valdares so attractive.

Inevitably, whenever she came out here, her mind returned to the question of Don Julio and his determination to gain possession of Ramón's property, and it was almost as if her thoughts of him had conjured up the man himself when she saw the distant figure of a man on a horse lower down the hill.

At the sight of him her heartbeat increased in pace until her head pounded with it, and Dorcas sighed at her own impressionability. Where the hill sloped downwards and the line of trees curved inwards, it gave a view of the lower ground and it was possible to see the solitary rider coming along in the shimmering heat of the sun.

His black head was exposed to the heat and his eyes unshielded from the glare and he blended with the landscape as if he was part of it. Mounted on a magnificent golden brown stallion, he looked as impressive as any proud *conquistadore*, and Dorcas wished she had the strength of will to turn back to the villa and avoid meeting him again.

Then he disappeared again behind the trees and was lost to her sight for as long as it would take him to ride to the higher ground where she was herself. It was a strange sense of anticipation that curled in her stomach as she walked, waiting for him to appear again, and she had never stopped to ask herself why she experienced it each time she saw him.

Neither did it occur to her to wonder why he rode along that boundary each day, or why she continued to walk there every day when she knew there would be a chance of seeing him. She would have immediately dismissed as ridiculous any suggestion that either of them did so for any other motive than convenience.

She had walked only a few yards when he came into view again, and she glanced, as she always did, through the concealment of her thick lashes at the tall arrogant figure on the horse, clear and solid, outlined against the bright sky and the distant hills.

Long, powerfully muscled legs did as much to control his mount as the strong brown arms and hands exposed by a short-sleeved shirt, so white that it made him appear as dusky-skinned as his

Moorish ancestors must have been. A proud head on the strong column of neck presented in profile a long, hawkish nose and a chin that matched the unrelenting set of the wide, straight mouth. A bloodthirsty corsair, she had imagined him, and she saw no reason to change her opinion on closer inspection.

With that dividing line of trees between them it would have been easy to avoid acknowledging each other, but somehow they never had, and this morning was no exception. Dorcas saw his head turn in her direction as he went by, his eyes narrowed because, where he was in the full brightness of the sun, she must have appeared as barely more than a small shadowy figure among the trees.

'Buenos días, señorita!' The deep, quiet voice carried well, but was flattened by the open air and the surrounding trees, and Dorcas inclined her head, as she always did in response to the greeting.

'Buenos días, señor!'

Usually after that brief and formal exchange he passed on, sometimes spurring his horse to greater efforts and galloping across the wide pasture towards the stables and the paddock in the distance. Today, however, he reined in the brown stallion and held him taut on a tight rein, with his elegant head and neck arched, his restless hooves stamping on the dry earth impatiently. Then sharp spurs urged him into the shade of the trees until he hovered near Dorcas nervously.

Don Julio sat for a moment, looking down at her in silence, his dark eyes making a slow and disturbing survey of her features until she felt as if she wanted to turn and run. 'If I might have a moment of your time, *señorita*,' he said quietly, and for a second Dorcas simply stared at him in surprise.

It was the second time in three days that he had addressed himself to her, and she wondered if that brief meeting in the church of San Julio had set a precedent. Dorcas half-smiled, not quite sure how forthcoming she should allow herself to be. She disapproved of him and his ruthless quest after her half-brother's land, and she had never made any secret of it, but somehow it was difficult to prevent that small half-smile from showing itself.

'Of course, Señor Valdares,' she said in as cool a voice as she could muster in the circumstances. 'Just as long as you don't intend asking me anything about buying my brother's property!'

To have been so bluntly outspoken was, of course, bad manners, and she immediately regretted the impulse that had prompted her to say it, but there was little she could do about it now. Briefly a frown appeared between the black brows and she was subjected to a look that would have daunted a less lively spirit than Dorcas, and his voice had a steely edge to it when he answered her.

'I would not even consider consulting you about a matter that is of concern only to myself and Señor Lorenzo, *señorita*,' he informed her coolly. 'Such matters do not concern women, and particularly not such a—*perdón*—such a young woman.'

His reference to her youth, although made in coolly polite terms and with no suggestion of malice, stung Dorcas's pride, and her eyes blazed at him for a moment until she recovered her self-control. Then she lifted her chin and regarded him for a second down the length of her small nose.

'I may be considerably younger than my brother and yourself, *señor*,' she told him in a small tight voice, 'but I am personally interested when someone, *anyone*, is trying to take his land from him against his wishes!'

It would have been so much more satisfying if he in turn had been angry, but instead he merely regarded her with those glittering dark eyes and ignored the provocation she offered. 'I will not discuss such matters with you, *señorita*,' he said quietly. 'It is of Señor Montez that I wished to speak.'

Once again Dorcas stared at him in disbelief. He denied her the right to an interest in her brother's affairs, but apparently saw nothing wrong in his own interest in her friendship with Rafael. She half turned away, shaking her head to let him know that Rafael was a subject *she* was not prepared to discuss.

'There is nothing to speak about,' she said shortly, and moved away from the proximity of the brown stallion, giving a wide berth to his impatiently tossing head.

'Señorita James!'

The imperious voice followed her through the thin line of trees, but Dorcas ignored it and walked on, her legs feeling dismayingly weak as she listened for the following snort of the stallion. She heard nothing of the horse, but a moment later the man himself appeared beside her, tall and arrogant, one hand holding the reins, the other placed with careful restraint on her arm.

'It is important that I speak with you, *señorita*,' he said, still in the same quiet tones. 'You will do well to listen to me for your own sake.'

The touch of those long brown fingers on her arm burned her flesh like fire and she felt the agitated hammering of her heart at her ribs as she licked her lips anxiously, summoning the courage to look up into his face and deny him the right to interfere in her affairs. 'I can manage my own life perfectly well, Señor Valdares,' she said in a light, husky voice. 'I don't *need* your help, and you have no right to even mention my friendship with Señor Montez.'

For a moment he did not move or speak but stood with his fingers still curled about her soft skin, his dark eyes looking down at her with a strangely anxious expression in their depths that puzzled her. '*Muy bien*,' he murmured softly at last. 'If you will not listen, *señorita*, then I will speak to your brother.'

'Ramón?' She looked startled and he nodded, his hand at last withdrawn but leaving its warm imprint still on her flesh.

'I have attempted to deal with the matter in the way I know that Englishwomen expect to be treated,' Don Julio informed her coolly, 'but since you are firmly resolved not to listen to me, *señorita*, then I shall be obliged to see your brother and let him know he should forbid you to see Montez again.'

'Forbid me to——' Dorcas stared at him unbelievingly, then she shook her head slowly, trying to convince herself that it was not all some curious dream. 'Ramón wouldn't dream of forbidding me to see Rafael—it's no concern of his who I see, and he wouldn't dream of interfering!'

'Of no concern?' He looked genuinely puzzled for a moment, the black brows drawn close in a frown, then he narrowed his eyes and tightened that firm mouth even more. 'You will surely not defy the strict instruction of your brother, Señorita James,' he said in a cold, stern voice. 'No young woman is surely allowed such complete control of her behaviour!'

'My life is my own,' Dorcas insisted, her eyes sparkling with the justice of her cause. 'No one has the right to interfere, not even Ramón—certainly not you, Señor Valdares! Now if you'll excuse me I'll have to get back. I have a luncheon appointment with Rafael Montez!'

'*Caramba!*' The oath was brief and forceful and Dorcas swung round instinctively when she heard it, her eyes blinking in surprise at the vehemence in his voice, but he was already shaking his head as if he regretted the moment of violence. 'I should explain to you, *señorita*,' he said in a tight, hard voice. 'Señor Montez——'

'Is no concern of yours!' Dorcas interrupted without hesitation. Her mouth was set stubbornly and she would have turned away from him again, but he swore again, even more virulently, and before she could walk out of reach his free hand caught her. She was pulled violently against the unyielding masculine hardness of his body with a force that drove the breath from her, and her hands curled involuntarily into fists which she used to pound hard at his chest, struggling frantically to escape.

Almost contemptuous of her struggles, he held her in one strong arm, and contact with that unyielding, masculine strength added panic to her fight to be free and stirred her emotions into chaos. His dark features were only inches from hers and she felt herself compelled to look up into them, to meet the bright glittering gaze that studied her with fierce intensity.

'It is not my duty to instil good manners into you, *poca tizón*,' he said in a voice that was harsh and flat with temper, 'or I would do so with pleasure!' The words were breathed warmly against her mouth and she felt herself trembling violently in that relentless grip. Then as suddenly as he had snatched her into his hold he realeased her, his wide, straight mouth curled derisively at her obvious panic. 'I will contact Señor Lorenzo and inform him of the situation,' he informed her shortly. 'Now go while I still remember that you are no more than a child!'

Trembling and too shaken to say or do anything, Dorcas turned away, stumbling as she turned, then fled as fast as she could with dignity, up the hill towards Casa de las Rosas, her heart thudding relentlessly hard in her breast. Never, never would she forgive him for that last derisive remark, and not for anything would she have Ramón know that he had made it.

She was still shaking like a leaf when she got back to the house and Ramón, who was about to start his work for the day, looked at her curiously when she came into his office. Her cheeks were bright and angry and a blaze of anger gave her blue eyes a dark, sparkling look that he viewed with some speculation.

'I thought I'd better warn you,' Dorcas told him

without preliminary, 'Don Julio Valdares is coming to see you—or at least he's going to contact you!'

Ramón looked far less perturbed by the information than he should have done, Dorcas felt, and frowned at him. 'Did he tell you so, *pequeña*?' he asked gently, and Dorcas nodded.

'I think you ought to know, Ramón,' she said, 'that Don Julio intends to try and interfere in my—my friendship with Rafael Montez, he has admitted as much!'

Now Ramón frowned, though more in curiosity than anger, she realised, and he studied her for a moment with his dark eyes questioning. 'Why should he do such a thing, Dorcas?' he asked, and reached for her hand, drawing her closer to him as he sat in the chair at his desk, his crippled legs concealed by its panelled sides. 'Is there perhaps something about Rafael Montez that I do not know?'

'You know as much about him as I do,' Dorcas told him, a hint of reproach in her voice for his attitude. 'And I think you might support me against a stranger interfering in what doesn't concern him! Don't you trust me, Ramón?'

'Of course I trust you,' Ramón said quietly, his strong fingers stroking hers soothingly as he spoke. 'But I know so very little about Rafael, *pequeña*, it could be that Don Julio knows something we do not and wishes to warn us.'

'But it has nothing to do with him!' Dorcas objected. 'Why should he take it upon himself to—to poke his oar in, when he has no possible interest or concern in our affairs?'

'As a neighbour perhaps he sees it as his duty, if

there is something—undesirable about Rafael Montez.' A long hand lent all sorts of meaning to the suggestion. 'Although I have heard nothing,' he added, and Dorcas shook her head slowly, suddenly uneasy.

'You know the family he comes from,' she reminded him. 'Surely you know if they're—respectable or not. You said they were wealthy, didn't you?'

Ramón's mouth smiled a little ruefully and he shook his head while he stroked her fingers gently. 'To be wealthy is not automatically to be respectable,' he told her. 'I know nothing about the family, *niña*, only that they are wealthy and live in San Bartolo.'

Dorcas said nothing for a moment, but looked down at the strong, gentle hands of her brother, wondering if Julio Valdares' warning would cause him to intervene in her relationship with Rafael. She had been so sure when she told Don Julio that Ramón would not interfere, but his present attitude gave her food for thought, and she was not at all happy about it.

'You don't trust my judgment?' she suggested, after a while, and Ramón smiled as he shook his head.

'I question only that you are a little young for your judgment to be infallible, *pequeña*,' he told her gently. 'We should perhaps listen to what Don Julio has to say, hmm?'

'You can listen,' Dorcas told him, leaving no doubt as to her own opinion. 'I'm seeing Rafael for lunch.'

Ramón's dark eyes surveyed her for a moment

in silence, then he smiled ruefully and shook his head at her. 'You do not like to yield your opinions, do you, Dorcas?' he asked softly, and she looked at him briefly with uncertain eyes.

'I—I can't believe I'm wrong about Rafael,' she said, and wished she could sound more positive.

'We shall see,' was all the consolation that Ramón offered, and she nodded her head vaguely as she walked to the door of his office, turning to look at him when something came to mind.

'What does—' She struggled briefly with the Spanish words. 'What does *poco tizón* mean?' she asked, and Ramón's dark brows flickered swiftly upwards, a hint of amusement lurking in his eyes as he looked across at her.

'Who calls you little firebrand?' he asked.

Dorcas blinked at him for a moment then turned again and went out. 'Don Julio Valdares,' she said over her shoulder. 'You might have known!'

It was unlike Dorcas to sit quietly while they drove along towards San Julio, and once or twice she knew Rafael glanced at her curiously, so that she hastily passed some trivial opinion of the countryside. But Rafael would not be satisfied with such evasive tactics for very long, she guessed, and glanced at him from the concealment of her lashes, trying desperately hard to convince herself she couldn't be wrong about him.

He was a few years older than she was, possibly about twenty-four or five, and quite remarkably good-looking. His hair was black and lightly curled and his eyes as black and glittering as jet, set between thick black lashes. His mouth held a hint

35

of sensuality in its lower lip, but his usual expression was one of frank amiability rather than passion and Dorcas wondered if she could have been wrong all this time. She couldn't tell him about Don Julio's proposed visit to her brother, of course, but she would like to have the matter settled one way or the other.

There was a small restaurant that they liked just off the main street in San Julio, and it was there that Rafael took her again, the proprietor greeting him as a valued customer. Sticking to dishes she knew, Dorcas ordered an omelette first and followed it with *pinchitos árabes*, which was cubes of mutton, highly seasoned and grilled. With her appetite almost completely satisfied she settled for a little fresh fruit to finish with, and smiled at Rafael over a glass of clear red Valdepeñas.

She was feeling oddly maudlin and she had drunk very little of the wine, so she could not blame it on to that. 'Thank you, Rafael,' she said quietly, and he raised a brow as he looked at her.

'Why do you say it so, Dorcas?' he asked. He reached for her fingers and gently lifted them in his, but made no more extravagant gesture, like raising them to his lips, he simply held her hand and looked at her curiously. 'Is something wrong?' he asked.

Dorcas shook her head, gently disengaging her hand and gazing down into her empty wine glass. There was nothing wrong, she mustn't let there be, for she enjoyed Rafael's company and she couldn't believe he was anything other than a handsome and well-mannered young man who liked taking her out.

'No, there's nothing wrong,' she assured him, and managed to smile more convincingly this time. 'It's the wine, I think,' she laughed. 'I've had too much and it's making me a bit sad.'

'Oh, Dorcas, how can you be sad?' He reached for her hand again and this time he did press his lips briefly to her fingers. 'It is a lovely day and we have a good *almuerzo, si*? So why could you be sad?'

'I don't know.' She did nothing about the long brown fingers that held hers so gently, but still looked down into her glass, trying to find words to express her mood, as much for her own benefit as for Rafael's. 'Somehow—somehow everything seems different.'

'Different?' he echoed her, his eyes searching her face for reasons. 'How so—different, Dorcas?'

For a moment Dorcas said nothing, then she looked up at him and slowly shook her head. If only she could ask him about himself without giving him any clue as to her reasons for asking, but it was not easy and she was so afraid of offending him. 'I don't know,' she confessed at last, and Rafael smiled.

'Of course nothing is different,' he said confidently. 'I am here, you are here and it is a beautiful day! How can anything be different, huh?'

Only too willing to be convinced, Dorcas took her cue from him and after a second or two smiled and shook her head more firmly. 'Of course nothing's different,' she agreed. 'How could it be?'

Rafael's black eyes glowed in a way that they never had before and he took her hand again, more firmly this time, and more confidently it seemed to

Dorcas, his fingers curling strongly round hers and squeezing, while he leaned across the width of the small table and gazed into her eyes.

'It can be different only if you want it to be, *mi amar*,' he said softly. 'Is that what you want, hmm?'

Dorcas was taken by surprise by the sudden change, although she should not have been, she told herself. She had always seen Rafael as much more passionate than he had been so far, and she should not have been surprised that he was now showing signs of living up to her expectations. Although whether she wanted it that way at this particular moment was in some doubt.

'I—I don't think I do, Rafael,' she said, and wondered how she could possibly sound so breathless. 'I like the way we are, I enjoy being with you, but——'

'But you do not want me to be in love with you!' Rafael's black eyes had a glittering look suddenly. 'I have sensed this from the first time we met, Dorcas, and I have been very patient, I think, but you are a very beautiful woman and I am a man—I am a Spaniard! Would you have me follow you around like a—a *perro* for always?'

'Oh, Rafael, please!' Dorcas shook her head, her eyes wide, afraid that the change she had feared had come about when she least expected or wanted it. Her English reticence shrank from a public display of passion, and she hated to think of him making a scene there, in the restaurant. 'Please don't be angry,' she begged. 'I—I'm sorry I spoke as I did, but I—oh, I don't know *what* I want to happen!'

'Dorcas!' He raised her hand to his lips and pressed them to her palm, his eyes like black coals as he gazed across at her. 'I do not mean to make you do something you are unwilling to do—but you do not dislike me, I know you do not, *mi hermosa*! Will you deny it?'

'Of course I don't deny it,' Dorcas agreed anxiously. 'But I *like* you. Rafael, I'm not sure if I feel anything more strongly for you at the moment, that's all.'

For a moment he said nothing more, but held her hand in his, his eyes searching her face for some sign of relenting, then he shook his head slowly. 'Ah, *claro*!' he said at last. 'The English take time to decide, huh?' Expressive shoulders shrugged resignedly and he smiled, a mere crooking of his mouth at one corner as he played gently with her captive fingers. '*Muy bien, mi hermosa*, I will be patient for a little while longer.'

'Thank you, Rafael!'

He laughed softly and raised her fingers to his lips again. 'That is how we started all this!' he said quietly. 'Are you still sad, Dorcas?'

Whether she would have agreed or not, Dorcas was in two minds, but as she looked up to answer him her eyes were caught by another customer just being seated by the proprietor, and she stared for a moment, then bit her lip hard. She must have visited the little restaurant a dozen times with Rafael, but never before had she seen Julio Valdares there, and his presence now gave her a strangely guilty feeling.

'Dorcas?' Rafael was looking at her curiously, and at that moment Don Julio also looked across at her and she hastily lowered her eyes before that steady dark gaze. Curious, Rafael turned his head and looked over his shoulder at the newcomer, then swiftly turned back. *'Madre mia!'* he murmured harshly, and clenched his hands tight on the table.

His reaction stunned Dorcas for a moment and she simply stared at him, her eyes wide and puzzled, then she reached out and touched his hand, seeking explanations, her heart hammering urgently suddenly. 'Rafael, what's the matter?' she asked, and he shook his head.

'Don Julio Valdares,' he said confirming her worst suspicions. 'I have never before seen him here—why does he come now? Tell me, why does he have to come now?'

'I—I don't know,' Dorcas said quietly, her eyes sparing another hasty glance for the tall figure at the corner table. 'Why does it matter if he's here, Rafael?'

For a moment he made no answer, but she could see that he was thinking hard and she wondered what on earth could be causing him so much heart-searching. 'He seldom comes into San Julio even,' Rafael mused, his brows drawn together in a worried frown. 'He comes only to Mass and never to *un restaurante*, why is he here now, huh? *Dios!* Why is he here?'

'Rafael!' Dorcas's hand was trembling as she reached out to touch his and he did not cover her fingers as she half expected he would, but drew back his hand and sat with both his hands clasped together against his tight lips, his brows drawn darkly.

Then suddenly he looked across at her and for a moment simply looked at her with steady, speculative eyes until at last he shook his head. 'Why should it matter?' he asked, and laughed softly as he shook his head. '*Madre mia*, why does it matter? We are friends, *si*? We lunch together and we like to drive together, *si*?'

'We do,' Dorcas agreed, not only curious but wary too, made so by something in his manner. It was almost as if he was rehearsing a speech, an explanation, and she felt her heart pounding urgently in her breast as she glanced again at Don Julio Valdares. 'Rafael—' Again her eyes were drawn to that strong dark face, now bent over a menu, and she shook her head. 'Rafael, why does it matter if Don Julio sees you with me?'

'It does not matter,' Rafael insisted. 'I have said it does not matter, Dorcas.'

'But it does,' Dorcas argued quietly. 'It matters to you, Rafael, you made that obvious, and I can't think why you mind him seeing you with me. I wish you'd tell me.'

For a moment Rafael said nothing, his long hands toyed with the stem of his wine glass until Dorcas could have snatched it from him in her impatience, then he looked up at her again and smiled ruefully. 'I do not like him,' he said frankly. 'I do not like him at all, *mi hermosa*, and he—he is such a powerful man that I hesitate to anger him.'

'Anger him?' She gazed at him for a moment frowning. 'Why should it anger him that you take me to lunch? I know he doesn't like me going out with you,' she added, 'he told me so, only this morning, and he threatens to tell Ramón something that he says will make him forbid me to see you again.'

41

His oaths were virulent and fortunately indecipherable to her, but she looked at him in wonder as he curled his hands again tightly on the top of the table. Then he looked at her with eyes that speculated on her reaction, reaching out for her hands again. 'Dorcas,' he said, 'there is something —something that perhaps I should have told you, but——' An expressive shrug made his excuses for him. 'I must tell you now before Valdares tells your brother.'

'Rafael, if you——'

He silenced her with a finger on her lips and smiled ruefully. 'For several years now,' he said, 'it has been understood that I marry—a certain lady, when she reached the age of twenty-one years. This year she attains that age and——' Again that expressive shrug, and Dorcas stared at him.

'You—you're engaged to be married?' she whispered. 'But why—why didn't you tell me, Rafael? How could you go on seeing me all this time and not tell me a thing like that?'

'Because it is something I am obliged to do!' Rafael said harshly. 'Not something I wish to do, that is why I did not tell you!'

'I see.' Dorcas looked down at her hands, and felt very small and uncertain suddenly. Then without quite knowing why she looked again at Don Julio Valdares and thought of how he had tried to warn her of this. It *had* been for her own good, as he said, and she had refused to listen, but Ramón would listen, and he would expect her to dismiss Rafael once and for all from her life. Nothing less would satisfy Spanish honour.

'Dorcas!' Rafael took her hands again, his black

eyes huge and appealing, almost irresistible. 'Can you not see how I feel? The betrothal is to be made public within a month, but until then I could perhaps—escape from it, if the circumstances were right.'

Dorcas stared at him for a moment, her heart hammering urgently, foreseeing danger here if she allowed herself to be too easily persuaded. 'Rafael——' she frowned anxiously, 'do you—do you *want* to escape?'

'*Claro, mi amar!*' His black eyes glittered and he gripped her hands tightly. 'It was none of my doing, this *esponsale*!'

Still confused and not quite believing, Dorcas shook her head. 'You—you mean you weren't consulted?' she asked.

'I was, *si*,' he admitted. 'But how can a boy know what he will want in a few years' time? I was too young to know my own feelings! Valdares and my father wanted it, and I was not averse at the time to marrying Elena.'

'Don Julio Valdares?' Dorcas stared at him, her brain spinning wildly and unable to grasp everything at once. 'But—but how can it possibly concern him?'

Again Rafael's elegant shoulders shrugged an explanation. 'Who else?' he asked resignedly. 'She is his niece!'

CHAPTER THREE

NOTHING could ever be quite the same again, Dorcas realised that the moment Rafael told her about his betrothal to Don Julio's niece. No matter how unwilling a fiancé he professed to be, the fact remained that he was engaged to the girl, Elena Valdares, and there was little to be done about it. She knew without doubt that Ramón would frown on any further association, once he knew about it, and yet she hated to think of never seeing Rafael again.

If the engagement had been arranged between two young people, too young to realise what they were getting into, it did not seem right that they should be held to the agreement, but in Spain such an arrangement would be hard to break. Don Julio, for one, would be a hard man to convince, as he had already shown by trying to warn Dorcas about continuing with her association.

Although she blamed Rafael for not telling her about his fiancée, she could at the same time sympathise with him for feeling trapped. She would like to do something about helping him, but it was not something she could do without taking a great many chances and offending a number of people, including her brother.

Rafael drove her as far as the gates of the *patio*, as he always did, then turned in his seat before she

44

had the opportunity to do or say anything. He placed a hand on her arm and his eyes watched her anxiously when she turned towards him, one finger tracing the smooth line of her upper arm. He said nothing for a moment, but silently contemplated his moving finger.

'Will you see me again, Dorcas?' he asked at last, and the tone of his voice betrayed how doubtful he was, so that Dorcas found it very hard to be as adamant as she knew she ought to be.

'I—I shouldn't,' she said in a small voice. 'It isn't really fair to ask me, Rafael, you know that.'

The black eyes looked at her steadily and there was a hint of challenge in their depths, as if he knew well enough that she was merely mouthing what convention would demand of her and not what she really felt. 'But you want to see me again, *mi amar, si?*' he suggested softly, and she nodded.

'You know I'd like to, Rafael,' she told him, 'but in the circumstances I don't think I should. You must try and understand.'

Rafael's good-looking features seemed much less youthful suddenly and his mouth twisted into a caricature of its normal smile. 'Oh, yes,' he said softly, 'I understand, *mi hermosa*! It is what Don Julio wants to happen and he will not rest until you—dismiss me!'

'Well, you *are* engaged to his niece,' Dorcas reminded him unhappily. 'You should have told me about it, Rafael!'

He frowned, his full lower lip pouting slightly as if he was unaccustomed to being blamed for anything he did. 'If I had told you, *chiquita*,' he said, 'you would not have come with me at all, and we should not have enjoyed these past weeks together. Would you have it so?'

It was a difficult question to answer honestly and Dorcas took time. 'I've enjoyed coming with you,' she admitted at last. 'But the fact remains that you *are* engaged to someone else and you should have told me. Even in England, where I know you think things are much more free and easy, matters like engagements are binding and are only broken by mutual consent.' She looked at him curiously for a second. 'Is your—is Señorita Valdares as unwilling to go on with it as you are?' she asked, and Rafael shrugged.

'Who knows?' he shrugged noncommittally. 'Such a thing has never been discussed or even considered.'

Dorcas was thoughtful for a moment. 'I—I wish I could meet her,' she said, and Rafael looked at her as if she had taken leave of her senses, although it was obvious she was quite serious about it. Meeting Elena Valdares could help her to judge what the other girl's reaction was likely to be. 'I mean it, Rafael,' she insisted.

'But it would not be possible!' he objected, and she knew from his frown that he would be opposed to the idea at any cost. 'How would you meet?' he asked. 'Where would you meet, *mi amar,* and who would introduce you? Could I take you to her and say—Elena, this is the woman I love?'

'Of course you wouldn't say that!' Dorcas denied hastily. 'Because it isn't true, Rafael, and you know it isn't!'

'*Madre mia!*' Rafael exclaimed passionately. 'Do you think I do not know my own feelings?' He

46

reached for her hands and held them tight in his own strong fingers, looking at her with those bright, glittering black eyes. 'Do you not feel for me as I feel for you?' he asked, his voice hoarse with suppressed passion. 'Do you not love me also, Dorcas?'

'Oh, Rafael, please!' She withdrew her hands and turned swiftly in her seat to open the door, but he was out of his own side and round the car so quickly that he stepped in front of her as she turned to close the door.

'Do not simply—walk away from me, *mi amar*!' he begged huskily. 'Promise that you will see me again—you do care for me, I know! Say you do, Dorcas!'

Dorcas could feel the rapid and uneasy thudding of her heart against her ribs and she sought hard for words that were gentle and understanding without being too encouraging.

'I do like you, Rafael,' she explained, 'but at the moment I'm not sure just how much. I'm fond of you, but I don't think I love you, and until I know for sure I won't—I can't be responsible for you breaking your engagement to Señorita Valdares, or for giving Don Julio the chance to blame me for it.'

'Dorcas!' He reached out for her, trying to pull her into his arms, something she had never had to cope with from him before, and she evaded him by stepping aside and pushing at him with her hands, although she did not walk away as she could have done, but stood beside the car.

'One of us has to think about your fiancée's feel-

47

ings,' she told him, and he frowned blackly in reproach.

'You are cruel!' he accused. 'How can you be so cruel, *mi amar*? Have I not been the most patient of men during the past weeks? Have I not refrained from saying the things I have wanted to say to you because you would not have wanted me to speak too soon?'

'I'm sorry, Rafael.' She felt suddenly quite tearful when she thought of not seeing him again, and he was watching her with those huge appealing black eyes. 'Your—your engagement——'

'*Madre de Dios!*' Rafael breathed piously, appealing to heaven for patience. 'Can you not understand how I am trapped by this—this *contrato*? Will you not help me, Dorcas—*por favor!*' The plea was irresistible and she hesitated only a second, then she shook her head in the vague uncertain way that showed she was willing to help but unsure how she could, and Rafael leapt at the opportunity if offered him. 'Dorcas, *mi amar!*'

'I—I don't see how I can do anything about it,' she said unhappily.

'Oh, if you wish to you can do so much!' Rafael told her eagerly. 'I will not be tied by this *contrato*, *mi amar!* I will tell them that I refuse to let you go, then how can they hold me to it?'

'Rafael——' She bit her lip, ready to withdraw the support he seemed so certain he had from her, but he dismissed the likelihood of her backing down with an airy hand, and laughed, his dark head thrown back and his excellent teeth showing white in the darkly handsome face.

Then he bent his head and pressed his mouth

48

over hers, drawing her into his arms at the same time. '*Te quiero, mi amante!*' He kissed her again, longer and more fervently, and Dorcas fought for breath as she put her hands to his chest and pushed him away.

'Rafael, I——'

'You will see me again, *si*?' he murmured persuasively, and Dorcas realised she was nodding her head almost without knowing she was doing it. She was pulled back into his arms again swiftly and enveloped in the warm, spicy scent of his aftershave when his mouth covered hers again. Releasing her with a soft laugh of triumph, he walked back to his seat and slid behind the wheel again.

'Rafael!'

Her cry was lost in the sound of the engine, and he waved an airy hand. '*Hasta mañana!*' he called as he let in the clutch and started to turn. '*Adios, enamorada!*'

It was the following morning, shortly after breakfast, that Ramón announced that he had an appointment to see Don Julio Valdares, and Dorcas heard it uneasily. After seeing Don Julio lunching in the same restaurant that she and Rafael used, she should have expected a swift move on his part—of course, he would see her being there with Rafael as a deliberate defiance of his advice.

He had threatened to see Ramón and he was evidently losing no time in doing just that. Not that she could blame him quite so much, she had to admit, now that she knew the full facts, but she still disliked the idea of his interfering in her life. If Rafael was to be believed, the arrangement had

49

been as much of Don Julio's making as anyone's, and it was typical of him that he objected to having his plans spoiled.

Ramón, she knew, would listen gravely to what he had to say and would judge as harshly as Don Julio did, for he was entirely Spanish, despite that fact that he was her half-brother. He would more or less repeat the advice that Don Julio had given her, though perhaps more kindly, and expect her to follow it, for he shared his neighbour's sense of propriety in such matters.

Dorcas was determined to be well out of call when the meeting took place, although it was unlikely that Ramón would humiliate her by making his advice public. She would take a book and stay in her room until Don Julio was safely out of the way.

With that in mind she had her book in her hand and was about to go upstairs when Mercedes came from the kitchen quarters to answer the door. It would have been easy enough to hurry on up and be out of sight by the time the visitor was admitted, but somehow she found herself lingering in the hall instead of fleeing and a moment later Don Julio Valdares stepped into the wide, airy hall.

Dorcas's heart thudded alarmingly when she saw the tall, rangy figure coming across towards her with long easy strides, adapted to Mercedes' shorter step, and her hands curled into a tight little ball over the book she carried. Never had any man had such an effect on her before, and she resented it as she always did, her chin instinctively lifting as he came nearer, and her eyes bright and challenging in the face of his dark-eyed scrutiny.

He was very formally dressed for the visit and she was bound to admire the way a light fawn suit fitted his whipcord body to perfection, a brown shirt and silk tie lending sombre flattery to his deeply tanned skin. His black hair was brushed back from his forehead, although part of that thick swathe that normally covered half his brow was already falling into place, and his dark eyes immediately picked on Dorcas's diminutive figure in the middle of the hall.

'*Señorita!*' He bowed formally, and paused beside her, while Mercedes hesitated, hovering just beyond them, uncertain, her dark eyes switching from one to the other, bright and speculating in the cool shadowy hall.

'*Buenos dias, señor!*' The greeting was as their greetings always were, formal and strictly polite, and for a wild moment, Dorcas felt like laughing. He had come to complain to her brother about her going about with his niece's fiancé—Ramón would be disappointed in her, possibly even angry when he discovered she now knew of his engagement, and yet here they were exchanging formal and polite greetings as if there was nothing wrong at all. It all seemed slightly crazy to her somehow, and she wanted to giggle, instead she looked down at the book she held and waited to see what else he would say.

'Are you now aware of the reason I am here, *señorita*?' he asked quietly, and Dorcas, fully aware that Mercedes spoke quite good English, nodded uneasily.

'I learned yesterday that Rafael is engaged,' she told him.

The dark eyes searched her face for a second before he spoke. 'Did you ask him to explain, Señorita James?' he asked. 'Or did he volunteer the information?'

'He volunteered it,' Dorcas said, a faint flush colouring her cheeks when she remembered her stunned reception of the news. 'I don't ask questions about people's private lives, Señor Valdares!'

'In this case you would have done well to ask questions, *señorita*!' he retorted swiftly, then eyed her speculatively for a moment. 'If you are now aware of the circumstances, then it is possibly not necessary for me to see your brother,' he suggested, and one dark brow flickered upwards. 'You will not, of course, be seeing Rafael Montez again?'

If only he had not asked that of her, it might not have been necessary for him to see Ramón, but she felt bound to answer truthfully, and after several seconds she admitted it.

'In the circumstances, I—I shall be seeing him again,' she said.

He said nothing for so long that she curled her hands tightly in her nervousness, and Mercedes hovered even more anxiously in the background, fully aware that there was a serious matter in the balance, and anxious for Dorcas to be discreet rather than defiant. Then Don Julio lifted his head and gazed at her down the length of that hawk-like nose, his eyes glittering with anger.

'Do you behave so, simply to defy me?' he asked at last in a harsh, cold voice. 'Or do you delight in being promiscuous, *señorita*? Are you perhaps trying to prove that you can persuade any man to defy the conventions of his country, ignore his responsibilities and insult his fiancée, simply to satisfy your taste for illicit romance?'

It was a harsh, cruel judgment and Dorcas felt the colour drawn from her face by its sting, glancing desperately at Mercedes who was attempting to melt into the shadows around her. Her voice was huskily deep and shook alarmingly when she answered him, and she felt as if there were tears only just a blink away as she looked up at that dark, implacable face.

'You have no right to speak to me like that,' she said. 'No right at all, Señor Valdares! Please remember that it wasn't until yesterday that I *knew* Rafael was engaged to your niece, and it was as much a shock as it would have been to anyone else —even a Spanish girl in the same position!' She could not resist the jibe and she saw the way his straight mouth tightened.

'A well brought up Spanish girl would not have become involved with a man in the circumstances you met Montez!' he hold her harshly. 'And you can scarcely claim to be an innocent dupe when you say you will see him again, Señorita James!' The black eyes glittered down at her challengingly. 'Is it that you find the Spanish male so irresistible?'

'Not *all* Spanish males, by any means!' Dorcas retorted, and her meaning was obvious.

She had expected the insult to anger him even further and she was trembling like a leaf as she faced him in the cool, silence of the hall, but instead she could have sworn that the glitter in his eyes owed as much to amusement suddenly, as it did to that formidable temper he had shown her. He studied her for a long moment in silence and she felt her legs as weak as water while she bore it, then he turned to Mercedes and spoke to her in rapid and incomprehensible Spanish.

'Si, señor!' Mercedes readily responded to his request to be taken to her employer. She seemed completely overawed by him, and it annoyed Dorcas to realise it.

'You're going to tell Ramón?' she asked as he turned to go, and he turned again and looked at her with raised brows.

'Since you seem unwilling to see reason, señorita,' he said quietly, 'you leave me little choice.'

'It's unfair!' Her objection sounded quite naïvely childish, she realised as soon as she said it, but she knew she would find it much harder to defy Ramón than she did Don Julio, and she had promised Rafael she would see him again. 'I—I've promised I'll see Rafael again,' she said. 'I—I can't break my word.'

The dark eyes held her steadily. 'And I cannot allow Rafael Montez to break his word to my niece,' he said quietly.

'But—' She hesitated. 'It—it was all—arranged! It wasn't as if it was a proper engagement, no one will be hurt by it if it's broken off!'

'Broken off?' His eyes narrowed and he swept his gaze over her flushed face searchingly. 'Is that what he has in mind, señorita?'

Dorcas's heart was thudding wildly in her breast and she felt again like crying. 'I—I don't really know,' she confessed, then shook her head earnestly. 'I—I don't want anyone to be hurt, señor, please believe that, but—oh, it's so difficult to know who to believe!'

'But you would rather believe Rafael, hmm?'
His voice was so much more gentle suddenly, and
she found it much harder to be defiant in the face
of it.

'He—he says it was arranged by you and his par-
ents,' she explained. 'He says he——'

'It was arranged at the request of both Elena, my
niece, and Rafael Montez,' Don Julio interrupted
quietly. 'They were in love with one another and
so it was agreed that when Elena was twenty-one
the betrothal would be announced.'

'But that's not as Rafael tells it!' Dorcas said anxiously, and he shrugged his broad shoulders.

'You may believe which of us you wish, *señorita*,'
he said quietly. 'Perhaps a little of both is the better answer.'

Dorcas was finding it hard to be so adamant now
and she looked up at him uncertainly while he
stood only inches away, his dark face watching,
waiting, disturbing her senses and her ability to
think clearly. 'I—I enjoy going out with Rafael,'
she said in a small, plaintive voice, and for a brief
moment she caught another glimpse of that deep,
dark laughter in his eyes.

'So you *do* have a taste for Spanish men!' he said.
The dark eyes looked at her for a moment with an
intensity that she found hard to bear. She hated to
think he saw her as nothing more than a footloose
and rather cheap little adventuress, and the possibility of it left her feeling more tearful than angry.
One black brow elevated into that swathe of dark
hair and his wide mouth curved briefly in a hint of
smile. 'Perhaps,' he suggested softly as he turned to

follow Mercedes, 'I might offer myself in place of Rafael Montez!'

Ramón was as disturbed as Dorcas expected him to be by the news of Rafael's engagement, and he sat looking at her across the width of his desk saying nothing—a silence that she found more disturbing than accusations would have been.

She had waited only a few minutes after she heard Don Julio's car depart, then gone down to see Ramón and learn just what she had been accused of. Ramón would be very hurt that she had kept him in the dark about Rafael being engaged, she knew, but she had somehow shied away from telling him for fear of his reaction and because she meant to see Rafael again no matter what was said. Now, of course, his recent visitor would have made the situation quite plain.

'*Tonta niña,*' Ramón said softly, shaking his head, and Dorcas sighed. 'Dorcas, did you not realise how very foolish you were being?'

'I didn't know about Rafael,' Dorcas insisted, anxious to be believed. 'I didn't know until yesterday, Ramón, you can't blame me for not knowing!'

'And now that you know?' Ramón asked quietly, and Dorcas stayed uneasily silent for a long moment before she replied. Those watching dark eyes reminded her uncomfortably of Julio Valdares and she wished she was able to comply with what she knew he wanted her to do.

She looked down at her hands where they rested on the edge of his desk. 'I—I've promised to see him again,' she said, and Ramón sighed.

'So Señor Valdares told me,' he said. 'I was very sorry to hear it, Dorcas, and I cannot think that you mean to do as you say. You were perhaps acting in defiance of a man you find—overpowering.'

'I defy anyone to tell me how to run my life,' Dorcas said, her voice shaky, despite her determination. 'I like Rafael as a—as a friend, Ramón, that's all. I've no intention of making any more of our relationship than that, no matter what Don Julio Valdares says!'

'Or what Señor Montez says?' Ramón asked softly, and she looked up hastily, shaking her head.

'Rafael—he's being rather silly about it at the moment,' she said, trying to make it sound less important. 'He doesn't really love me, of course, I know that. I think he simply finds a certain novelty in the idea of a blonde English girl at the moment, but he'll go back to Elena Valdares. He won't let her down, I'm sure of it!'

Ramón looked not only shocked but angry, his brows drawn into an unfamiliar frown as if he speculated on the future intentions of Rafael Montez. 'He has actually spoken to you of these matters?' he asked, in a voice so alien to his usual soft tones that Dorcas frowned anxiously. 'He has dared to tell you that he is—in love with you, when he is betrothed to someone else?'

'But I told you, he doesn't mean it, Ramón——'

'He had no right to even mention such things!' Ramón declared firmly. 'And you should have told him so immediately, Dorcas! You should also have told me and I could have dealt with Señor Montez in the appropriate manner!'

'But I *did* tell him he was wrong!' Dorcas insisted, almost in tears. It was a new experience for her to see her loving half-brother in the role of accuser, and she blamed Don Julio Valdares for the change, no matter if he did have right on his side.

Ramón watched her for a moment steadily, as if he did not quite follow her meaning. 'Can you mean that he pressed his attentions upon you when you were not willing?' he asked, and Dorcas shook her head hastily.

'Oh no, of course not!' she denied. 'It's simply that he—well, he doesn't believe me when I say I don't love him. He's convinced I'll change my mind and become serious about him.'

'And will you?'

Dorcas licked her lips, judging his reaction through the thickness of her lashes. 'How can I tell!' she asked, wishing she knew the answer to that herself. 'But I don't think so.'

'*Bien!*' Ramón sat for a moment thoughtfully studying his long hands where they lay on the desk in front of him. 'I regret most deeply that I cannot take you around myself,' he said at last. 'I would have enjoyed it, Dorcas, showing you my country, and in my company there would have been no fear of you being touched by—gossip.'

'I know, darling Ramón,' she said, reaching across the desk and impulsively squeezing his hands. 'I wish you could act as my escort too—we'd have a great time, and you could keep me out of mischief too, couldn't you?'

'Such mischief as Señor Montez?' Ramón suggested with a half smile, and he shook his head slowly. 'I could not bear to see you hurt, *mi poca hermana*,' he said softly, 'and I am afraid that is

58

what will happen with this—this *aventurero*.'

'I'll be careful, I promise,' Dorcas said seriously, and squeezed his hands again reassuringly. 'I won't let myself be swept off my feet, honestly.'

Ramón sat for some time, one hand at his chin, his dark eyes downcast and unfathomable, as if he had something of importance on his mind. Then he looked across at her again suddenly and searched her face before speaking. 'You spoke to Don Julio Valdares before he saw me, I believe,' he said, and Dorcas nodded.

Her heart was doing a sudden and rapid tattoo at her ribs, although there was no good reason for it. 'I saw him,' she agreed cautiously, and Ramón pursed his lips thoughtfully for a moment, his long fingers steepled together on the desk.

'Don Julio has made an offer to escort you to various places of interest, in my stead,' he said, speaking slowly, as if he chose his words carefully. 'If the suggestion meets with your approval, of course.'

Dorcas gazed at him for a moment in disbelief. It was true he had made that, as she thought, facetious remark about substituting himself for Rafael, but she had not for one moment taken him seriously. The thought of him having suggested it to her brother as a serious plan stunned her into momentary silence and she simply shook her head slowly.

'You—you surely can't be serious, Ramón,' she said at last, and he frowned.

'I am quite serious,' he informed her. 'Have you some objection to being escorted by Don Julio?'

'Well, of course I have!' she exclaimed. 'I—I dis-

59

like him intensely, you know that, Ramón!'

'I know that you are frequently proclaiming the fact that you dislike him,' Ramón agreed, and Dorcas stared at him.

'With good reason,' she retorted. 'He's trying to take your land away from you!'

Ramón's quiet smile got on her nerves as he quietly demolished her main excuse for refusing the offer. 'I have so far managed perfectly well to say no to such plans,' he said blandly. 'I can continue to do so for as long as it suits me, *pequeña*, without any need for you to carry on a personal vendetta with Don Julio about it.'

'I—I still don't have to like him,' she declared stubbornly. 'And—and anyway, he's older than I am, a lot older. At least fourteen or fifteen years!'

Ramón's mouth quirked at one corner, apparently amused by her determined argument. 'Would you have me feel like an old man, *niña*?' he asked gently. 'Don Julio is my own age, and I can assure you, my little sister, that apart from these useless limbs, I am far from decrepit!'

'Oh, darling, I know!' She gazed at him apologetically, wishing that the idea of being squired by Don Julio Valdares did not appeal to her so much. She didn't want to like the idea, but in her heart she had to admit she found it quite head-spinningly exciting. Her pulses were already racing wildly at the prospect and she felt far more excited then she ever had at the thought of an outing with Rafael. 'I—I wouldn't have thought Don Julio liked the idea of being in my company, any more than I relish being in his,' she suggested, and Ramón raised a brow as he looked at her.

'But you forget, *pequeña*,' he reminded her softly, 'Don Julio has a motive for making such an offer. He is very fond of his young niece and your continued association with Rafael Montez is likely to hurt the Señorita Elena, if it continues.'

'Oh yes, I see.'

Dorcas felt rather as if he had slapped her and, sensitive as ever to the tone of a voice, Ramón looked at her steadily for a moment. 'Does it not please you, *niña*,' he asked softly, 'that his reasons are not more personal?'

Surprised by his acumen but determined not to admit anything, Dorcas shifted uneasily. 'Nothing surprises me about Don Julio Valdares,' she retorted defensively. 'It was only to be expected that anything he did was to serve his own ends. The only surprise is that he can't see the danger of gossip in escorting a girl he scarcely knows—and alone! I'd have thought his Spanish propriety frowned on *that*!'

'As would mine,' Ramón told her quietly. 'A man of Don Julio's standing would not suggest such an arrangement. Doña Maria Valdares would accompany you wherever you went with Don Julio —you would be quite safe.'

For a moment Dorcas's heart stopped beating and she held her breath. 'Doña Maria?' she said in a small husky voice. 'He—he's married?'

'No, no, *mi chiquita*,' Ramón told her with a smile. 'Doña Maria is the mother of Don Julio— she would act as your *dueña*.'

'A *dueña*?' Dorcas laughed, intrigued with the idea of being treated like the traditional Spanish lady. 'It sounds like fun,' she decided, then pulled a face. 'Except that I should have to put up with Don Julio as well,' she remembered.

'And that you will not accept?' Ramón enquired gently.

Dorcas smiled, her eyes hidden by carefully concealing lashes. 'I've never had my dates arranged second-hand,' she said. 'I don't propose to start now —if Don Julio Valdares wants to take me out, he can ask *me*!'

CHAPTER FOUR

WHEN Rafael did not see her for a couple of days Dorcas suspected that his conscience might have been troubling him, although he had denied it when she made the suggestion, and claimed some pressing family business. In one way Dorcas was glad to have some time to herself, for it gave her the opportunity to consider her future relationship with Rafael—and that, she felt, needed a great deal of thought at the moment.

Neither she nor Ramón had said anything more about Don Julio Valdares' suggestion that he should take her out and about in Rafael's place, and she had seen nothing of the man himself, so that she felt rather unsettled.

When Rafael was not available to drive her, Dorcas took a taxi to wherever she wanted to go and she had one take her into San Julio to do some shopping. She liked visiting the little town whether shopping or not, and it provided the shops she needed as adequately as any other small town could have done.

For several weeks now she had had her eye on a rather delightful little figure of Saint Teresa with the idea of buying it to present to Doña Teresa on her name day. It was a little over a week now to the Saint's special day and she was afraid that if she left it any longer the figure would be bought by some eager tourist with an eye for its delicate beauty.

The proprietor of the little shop smiled his pleasure at her choice and handed it to her to examine with a few murmured words of appreciation. The pottery was cool and smooth in her hands and the saint's benign and placid face reminded her of her old friend in the church of San Julio, so that Dorcas needed very little more convincing that it was an ideal present for Doña Teresa.

She smiled at the man and nodded, exchanging the wrapped figurine for a surprisingly small number of *pesetas*, and left the shop well pleased with her purchase. Doña Teresa, she felt sure, would be touched by the gift, and she was fond enough of the old lady to want to please her.

The door of the little shop stood open to the bright, hot street and Dorcas turned as she stepped outside, smiling at the proprietor over her shoulder, and unaware of anyone else in the proximity of the doorway or the imminence of a collision. The figure of Saint Teresa was in one hand, wrapped in tissue and loosely held because one had the impression that she was so fragile she would crush if held too tightly. Instead she was swept from Dorcas's grasp by the force of the collision, and Dorcas cried out in her anxiety when her treasure crashed to the pavement.

'Oh no!'

She gazed down at the bundle of tissue on the hot pavement and blinked back the tears that sprang into her eyes at the sight of her precious gift, so quickly broken. There could be no doubt at all that it was broken, for the sound of its shattering had been self-evident, and the package now looked ominously crumpled where it lay at her feet.

She was on her knees in a moment, without even looking to see who was responsible for the disaster, taking up the pitiful fragments of pottery in her hands, heedless of the sympathetic looks of passers-by. Only Saint Teresa's bland and patient face remained intact, her robes were now no more than a few dark blue and white slivers of pottery among the soft tissue.

Male feet in soft leather shoes, and long legs crouched double to bring the culprit to pavement level, were all she could see, but they struck a disturbingly familiar note. Then a large brown hand reached down and laid the severed head among the ruins, and at last Dorcas looked up.

'This is most unfortunate, Señorita James!' he said, and the familiar voice struck her at the same moment as the dusky features of Don Julio Valdares became recognisable through her tears, and she clenched her hands tightly as she stood upright again, facing him.

'I might have known it was you!' she said bitterly, and looked down at the shattered figure of Saint Teresa again. 'It's completely ruined!'

No one else lingered to see what had happened, and for that at least Dorcas was thankful, for she hated the idea of making a fool of herself in public by crying over a broken pottery figure. No one else would understand how she had looked forward to giving it to Doña Teresa, least of all this hard, unyielding man facing her.

He too looked down at the fragments of Saint

Teresa and shook his head. 'I assume from your reaction that the figure had some special significance for you,' Don Julio said in his deep, soft voice. 'Can it not be replaced?'

Dorcas shook her head, unwillingly aware of the way her heart was responding to the sound of that voice, and to the shattering air of masculine self-confidence that emanated from him. One large hand now cupped her own two much smaller ones as well as the fragments of pottery and she felt her heart drumming wildly at her ribs at the touch of his fingers curled over hers.

'There isn't another one just like it,' she said in a small, plaintive and definitely accusing voice.

'I am sure there must be, *señorita*!' He looked into the little shop behind her. 'Such a place does not sell exclusive or expensive ornaments.'

'It was better than any of the others,' Dorcas insisted, growing angry over his apparent unconcern. 'I've had my eye on it for several weeks now, and just when I decide to buy it, you come along and break it! I could cry!' She looked up at him with defiance in her eyes. 'I suppose you think I'm silly to cry about a cheap pottery statue?' she suggested defensively, and he shook his head, slowly.

Unable to brush the tears from her eyes because both her hands were full, she looked up at him with them still clinging to her lashes, and hazily she saw him take a handkerchief from a pocket and fold it carefully. With one corner of it he gently brushed away the tears and regarded her for a moment before answering the accusation.

'Not if it is important to you,' he denied calmly. 'But it was foolish of you to carry it so carelessly if it was as precious as you claim, and certainly you have no reason to blame me for the accident.'

'But you charged into me!' Her voice was husky and it shook betrayingly when her senses responded to even that small attention.

He said nothing for a moment, but regarded her steadily, and Dorcas thought she detected as much resignation as anger in his eyes when she chanced a brief upward glance. Then the hand that held hers relinquished its hold slowly, almost reluctantly. 'I was passing when you turned in the doorway, then came out without looking where you were going, *señorita*,' he argued quietly. 'But since you insist that I am to blame for the loss of the figure, then I must replace it.'

Dorcas shook her head, seeing her accusation taking a completely unexpected turn. 'Oh, but I didn't mean you to do that!' she denied. 'It really isn't necessary, Señor Valdares!'

'You have stated quite clearly that you consider the fault was mine,' Don Julio told her coolly. 'Therefore it is fitting that I should replace the figure.' One large and unyielding hand was placed over her arm and Dorcas was loath to shy away from its touch too violently in a place as public as the main street of San Julio, although the pressure of those strong figures did alarming things to her self-control. 'Which saint had attracted you?' he asked, and Dorcas answered almost automatically.

'It was Saint Teresa.'

'Whose day is celebrated next neek,' he said, nodding his head as if he understood at last. 'Perhaps the figure was a gift for Doña Teresa?' he suggested, and Dorcas nodded agreement.

She felt slightly breathless with those strong brown fingers curled over her arm still. 'I—I saw it and liked it,' she told him. 'I thought Doña Teresa might appreciate it, coming from me.'

'I am sure that she will,' he agreed. 'But in the circumstances, *señorita*, perhaps I may be permitted to replace the figure with one that I have in my home—I am sure that it will be quite to Doña Teresa's taste.'

'Oh, but I couldn't let you do that!' Dorcas objected. 'I can't let you go to those lengths to replace a—a little pottery statue.'

'It is my wish to do so, *señorita*,' he replied coolly, and the curl of those strong fingers was playing havoc with her senses.

'But, Señor Valdares——'

'It is done,' he informed her adamantly, and the hand on her arm was withdrawn suddenly, leaving its imprint on her skin. He turned and inclined his head briefly only as he started to walk away from her. '*Hasta luego, señorita!*' he said coolly, and left Dorcas staring after his tall figure with her emotions chaotically disturbed. It was only after he had disappeared into the people crowding the narrow street that she realised he had said nothing more about his suggestion that he should take her out in Rafael's stead.

Whether her change of venue was deliberate, to avoid meeting Don Julio, Dorcas could not have said for sure, but the following day she walked instinctively in the opposite direction to that which she normally took, despite the fact that if offered much less shade.

The land this side sloped away much more sharply towards the village and the going was harder and more rough, although it still gave a breathtaking view of the surrounding countryside. She needed to watch her step as she walked down the hill and she missed the cool shade of the bordering trees, for it was quite unbearably hot in the sun, and she wore nothing on her head.

The little whitewashed *casetas* shimmered hazily in the heat at the bottom of the hill, and the arid earth of the erstwhile olive grove she walked in looked hard and yellow underfoot. In contrast the plane and eucalyptus trees on the far side spread delicious shade where she more usually walked and she was already regretting her change of plan.

A sleeveless dress of yellow cotton flattered the pale golden tan she had managed to acquire in the weeks she had been at Casa de las Rosas, and her legs were bare as they usually were, but she wished she had brought a hat, for her head was already throbbing with the heat and the sun's glare made her narrow her eyes against it.

The sudden spinning sensation she experienced was both startling and unexpected and she put a hand to her throbbing head and closed her eyes to shut out the glare of the sun. It was not the ideal place to have an attack of sunstroke, right out here in the middle of a deserted and derelict olive grove, and that was what was in store for her if she did not turn around and go back before she got any worse,

Again as she turned to face the upward climb back to the villa, a sharp spasm of pain made her clutch her head, and she swallowed hard on the flutter of panic that gripped her when she thought of how far from help she was if she did succumb.

Closing her eyes again, she put both her hands to her burning head and stood for a moment recovering her sense of balance. It was while she stood like that she heard the distinct thud of hooves on the hard dry ground, but she was so dizzy and confused that the significance of it did not yet occur to her.

It was only seconds later that the snorting impatience of one of Don Julio's spirited mounts made her turn swiftly, realising at last that the man she had taken such pains to avoid had caught up with her anyway. Her eyes closed again briefly when the movement brought a wave of nausea and she was not at all sure she could face him at a time like this.

'You——'

She had time to do no more than croak the one word of objection for his being on her brother's land, when dizziness overcame her again and an arm stretched out and caught her as she swayed. Pulled against a firm, masculine body that smelled tangily of after-shave and horses, she closed her eyes again for a second and pressed her face comfortingly to the broad chest so conveniently available.

'*Cuidado!*' Briefly she was held close, then another arm swept her up and she was carried over to one of the straggling old olive trees and laid gently down in its shade while Julio Valdares knelt beside her, one arm still supporting her, a hand brushing back the hair from her brow with unbelievably gentle fingers.

'I'm sorry!' She laughed shakily and tried to sit up, but a firm, hard hand held her back against his raised knee and the temptation to remain there was difficult to resist. But resist it she did, and sat herself up, her legs curled under her, looking up at last into that dark, uncompromising face. 'I think I must have had too much sun,' she said huskily, and wished that the hand on her brow would cease its ministrations. The touch was at once both soothing and disturbing, and she was finding it very hard to think sensibly.

'I saw you from across the *campo*,' Don Julio told her. 'You appeared to be unwell and I feared you might faint before I could reach you.'

His concern surprised her, although she was ready to admit that she could be misjudging him, and she found herself oddly pleased by it. 'There's no shade this side,' she said, as if explanation was needed for her change of venue. 'It was silly of me to come over here.'

His eyes went to the shiny fairness of her long hair and he shook his head. 'You should not walk in the full sun with nothing to cover your head,' he told her quietly, and Dorcas glanced involuntarily at his own black head.

'Why not?' she asked with a slightly shivery laugh. 'You do!'

His expression was pitying and he was shaking his head again. 'That is a foolish comparison, *niña*,' he told her, 'and I think you know it is. You are not a Spaniard and you are not yet sufficiently accustomed to our climate to walk in the sun without somehing on your head . . .'

The intimate sound of that '*niña*' did disturbing things to her senses, although she knew from Ramón's use of the word that it meant he was calling her a child—something she would normally have objected to most strongly. There was too much about the present situation that was disturbing and she fought as hard as she could against the effect it was having on her.

'Well, I think I'm recovered enough now to get up off the ground,' she said. 'I'll get up now, please.'

Dark eyes looked down at her anxiously and that disquieting hand brushed again over her damp forehead. It was obvious that he considered her still unwell and being the man he was, he said as much without hesitation. 'I think you should take more time to recover,' he stated firmly. 'A few more moments will help.'

'But I'm quite well now,' Dorcas insisted, 'and this hard ground isn't the most comfortable place to recover! I—I just felt a little dizzy for a moment, that's all.'

It was much too disquieting sitting there curled up on the dry ground with a man like Don Julio Valdares in such close proximity. One arm was still lightly supporting her shoulders and the warm palm of his hand rested on her bare arm, gently provocative against her skin. Being close to him in that way did nothing to diminish the throbbing in her head, and her heart too was hammering hard, almost in panic as she made another effort to get up.

He rose swiftly to his feet and reached down with his hands to help her, his strong fingers curling firmly over her wrists, but obviously reluctant about her moving. 'You are safe?' he asked, and Dorcas thought it was a strange way to ask, but when she nodded to assure him she staggered

drunkenly and would have fallen. Swiftly that
steadying arm was around her again and for a moment she yielded both to the dizziness that briefly
overcame her and to the comfort of his enfolding
arm.

'You are in too much hurry to stand on your
feet,' Don Julio insisted. 'You must rest a little
longer, then I will return you safely to your
brother.'

'Oh no, really!' Dorcas objected, drawing away
from him to prove how fit she was. 'I'm perfectly
all right now, Señor Valdares!'

He stood for a moment looking down at her, as if
he knew differently, but then he shrugged in the
resigned and expressive way of his race and turned
to gather up the reins of his horse again. To show
that he was not entirely convinced, however, he
slid his free hand under her arm and looked at her
in a way that challenged her to remove it.

'If you had not sought to avoid me,' he remarked
calmly, confident of his facts, 'you would not have
become affected by the heat. Why were you so foolish, *señorita*?'

It was not easy to deny he was right with those
strong fingers curled round her arm, and Dorcas
made only a token attempt. 'I—I wasn't trying to
avoid you,' she denied, and a dark brow shot swiftly
into the dark hair over his brow.

'You lie, I think, *niña*,' he said gently, and
smiled.

It was the first time she had ever seen him really
smile and the effect of it on those usually stern
features was startling. Fine lines appeared at the
corners of his eyes and they crinkled into slivers of

glittering jet, while his wide straight mouth showed strong white teeth against the dusky darkness of his features. He had never, in Dorcas's eyes, looked more like the Moorish corsair she had once imagined him, and the effect was to set her pulses racing even harder and arouse in her a curious desire to laugh with sheer delight.

She controlled her voice with difficulty as she answered him, as simply and sensibly as she could in the circumstances. 'It—it was difficult to know exactly what to do after yesterday,' she said, and again one black brow rose in surprise.

'*Cómo dijo?*' he murmured, and Dorcas tried to explain.

'I remembered you said something about replacing the figure that got broken yesterday,' she said. She moved away, out of reach of his hand, then turned and looked at him, meeting his eyes briefly before she hastily looked away again. 'I—I didn't want you to,' she said. 'It really isn't necessary for you to replace it, it wasn't very expensive.'

'But a gift is not judged by its value in *pesetas*,' he told her quietly. 'You bought the figure because you thought that Doña Teresa would like it, and I am sure you are right—but as you were convinced that I was responsible for its being broken then it is correct that I should replace it.'

'But not with one of your own!' Dorcas denied earnestly. 'I'd much rather you didn't do that!'

He shrugged as if there was little he could do about her wishes. 'It is what I shall do,' he told her implacably. 'I have decided, *señorita*.'

Dorcas frowned, her natural instincts rebelling against the arrogance of the decision regardless of her own feelings. 'And therefore I have no choice but to accept!' she said, her resentment evident in her voice and the lift of her chin as she looked at him. 'Is your word law, *señor*?'

He held her gaze steadily for a moment, then slowly and very deliberately wound the reins he held round one of the branches of the olive tree, and the very deliberation of his movements roused strange sensations in Dorcas's emotions. He took the two short steps necessary to bring him close to her, then stood for a moment looking down at her steadily. He was so close she could feel the vibrant warmth of his powerful masculinity enveloping her like an irresistible aura, and her mouth was suddenly dry. So close that another inch or two would have brought him into contact with her and the temptation to reach out and touch him was hard to resist.

'Is this why Rafael Montez finds you so hard to give up?' he asked in a strangely husky voice that sent little shivers of sensation trickling along her spine. 'Is it by challenge that you make him ready to give up so much for you, *poco atormentador?*'

Dorcas gazed at him silently, her eyes wide and unable to escape from that steady, challenging gaze. 'I—I don't know what you mean,' she said at last. 'I don't——'

'You know very well what I mean, I think, *señorita!*' he insisted in the same husky voice.

'No!' Dorcas shook her head, her long fair hair swinging about her face and neck. 'I go with Rafael because he asked me to, and because I like being with him—I don't *do* anything to make him stay!'

'*Condenación!*' Don Julio swore softly. 'I have

to believe it!' His eyes narrowed suddenly and he searched her face for a long moment before he spoke again. 'And me, *señorita*?' he said quietly. 'Has your brother told you of my suggestion?'

Dorcas felt her heart hammering at her ribs so hard she felt sure it must be audible to the man who stood so close. When Ramón had told her of Don Julio's offer to take her out in Rafael's stead she had received the information with mixed feelings. She had, if she remembered, told Ramón that she would go with him only if he asked her himself.

'Ramón told me about your—your offer to take me out sometimes,' she said slowly and carefully.

'And your answer, *señorita*?' He asked the question softly and Dorcas felt suddenly lightheaded again as she carefully avoided looking at him.

'I told Ramón that I might agree to go with you, but only if you—if you asked me yourself, Señor Valdares,' she said huskily, and for a moment his eyes searched her face, as if he was unsure of her reasons.

'The English way?' he asked at last, and Dorcas nodded.

'If you like,' she agreed.

He said nothing for a moment, then his wide mouth curved briefly into a hint of smile. '*Muy bien, señorita*,' he said softly. 'Then I ask you myself if you will come with me.'

The dark eyes held hers steadily for a long while, then Dorcas looked away. Something in her cried out to her to say yes, she would go with him, but Ramón's mention of a possible motive behind the invitation still lingered uneasily in the back of her mind, and she hesitated. Maybe Ramón was right and his only reason for wanting to escort her was to enforce a break with Rafael Montez, and if it was she would refuse him out of hand, regardless of the clamouring desires of her own emotions.

Her blue eyes gazed at him searchingly for a moment before she asked her question, then she licked her lips anxiously. 'I—I'd like to know *why* you want to take me out, Señor Valdares,' she said, and quaked inwardly when she saw the swift dark frown that formed between his brows. 'Is it—is it simply because you want to stop me going with Rafael, for your niece's sake? Is that your reason?'

'I cannot believe you asked such a question of Rafael Montez,' he said in a cold, angry voice. 'Why then do you ask it of me?' His mouth looked tight-lipped and cruel and he was more angry than she had ever seen him, so that she instinctively shook her head in a vague uneasy way. 'Why?' he demanded. 'Did you ask him for reasons?'

'I don't trust you!'

There was more despair than anger in her response, but he could not have known that, and before she could realise it herself, he reached out his hands for her. She was pulled across those few dividing inches and swept into contact with the steely power of his body with a violence that brought a cry of protest from her. His arms bound her with a strength she could do nothing to combat and, after a brief glimpse of the fury in his eyes, the dark face completely filled her vision and his mouth descended on hers with such force that her head was thrust back against the iron hand that spanned the back of her neck and twisted tight into her hair.

Nothing she had ever known in her young life had prepared her for such an assault as this and for several panic-stricken seconds Dorcas beat at him with her fists, a protest he ignored, perhaps even failed to notice in the fury of his own passion. There was nothing tentative or tender in the way he kissed her, but the sheer brutal determination to dominate, and her lips stirred silently under his mouth, trying to cry out, to catch a breath before her heart broke with the urgency of its beating.

Slowly the pressure of his mouth eased until she could draw short, erratic breaths that fluttered anxiously while she lay limp and no longer struggling against the broadness of his chest. Her hands stroked unconsciously over the smooth thin jacket he wore, and she tried hard to think, to bring herself back to reality.

Julio Valdares' black eyes looked down at her for a moment, a bright unfamiliar glow in their depths, then suddenly she was free, put away as ruthlessly as she had been forced into that shattering scene, and she trembled as he let his hands fall, leaving their hard, firm imprint on her flesh, burning like fire.

Dorcas opened her eyes at last, feeling herself unsupported, and found him standing back in the deeper shade of the olive tree, its twisted grey branches casting even darker shadows onto that dark, autocratic face, the eyes glittering between narrowed lids as he looked at her with an intensity that made her shiver.

'Llo siento, señorita!' The brief and formal apology sounded strangely flat and unemotional after the violent emotions of the last few minutes, and

Dorcas merely shook her head vaguely to deny the need for it.

Her head ached dully and she could not have said for certain which was the main cause for it. The effect of the sun on her uncovered head, or that fierce, savage assault on her senses. She glanced at Julio Valdares through the thickness of her lashes, studying those dark, implacable features with a new awareness.

Her body still tingled from its contact with the savage masculinity of his, and her mouth felt warm and trembling, bruised by the ferocity of his kiss. She had been kissed before and until now she had thought Rafael's kiss the most blood-stirring experience of her life, but with his violent fierceness Julio Valdares had aroused new and disturbing sensations in her that she found difficult to cope with yet.

His apology seemed something of an anti-climax compared to the upheaval her own emotions had suffered, and she gazed at him for a moment uncertain what to say or do. Don Julio's dark eyes still remained fixed firmly on her trembling mouth and it was hard to think calmly under such a scrutiny.

Then Dorcas licked her lips with the tip of her tongue and smoothed a trembling hand over her fair hair. 'I—I think I'll go back to the house,' she said, and her voice sounded small and shaky.

'*Señorita!* Dorcas!' His voice recalled her as she turned away and she did not turn back but merely stood still, her heart still pounding heavily in her breast. He came no nearer, but spoke from where he was, his voice deep and quiet and still able to create disturbances in Dorcas's senses. 'You are unwell from *insolación*,' he reminded her. 'May I not accompany you to your brother's house?'

Dorcas half turned, looking at him over her shoulder, her eyes meeting his only briefly. 'I think I can manage alone, thank you, Señor Valdares,' she said, and would have turned back, but something in his manner, in the depth of his eyes, held her.

'*Hasta mañana, señorita,*' he said softly, and Dorcas did not even trouble to deny that they would meet tomorrow—somehow it seemed inevitable.

CHAPTER FIVE

As she sometimes did after dinner, Dorcas took a gentle stroll with Doña Teresa in the gardens, enjoying the cool of the evening and the thousand and one wonderful heady scents of flowers and trees. Roses and magnolias hung heavy in the evening air, and there was a huge yellow moon that Dorcas gazed at every so often in wonder, marvelling that it could be the same she had seen in England, its golden light adding to the general headiness of the atmosphere.

Sometimes they talked quietly, at others they simply enjoyed their surroundings, exchanging no more than a few words. Dorcas had said little to either Doña Teresa or to Ramón about her encounter with Don Julio, and then only to tell them that she had been briefly overcome by the heat of the sun and he had come to her assistance.

Both of them, she thought, had been more curious about the behaviour of Don Julio in coming to her rescue than in her own condition, and their interest gave her an uneasy sense of anticipation which she could not explain. Not that they had been unconcerned about her, but an hour or two in the cool of her room had been enough to dispel the effect of the heat and she felt as well as ever she had by the time she came downstairs to dinner that evening. The disturbing effect of Julio Valdares' kiss would take longer to shake off, but that was something only she could cope with.

The cool voice of the fountain tinkled softly, competing with the quiet, persistent chirrup of the *grillos* in the shrubbery, and a light breeze stirred the palms like huge fans against the blue velvet sky. Until the moment when she saw Rafael by the gates of the *patio*, Dorcas felt relaxed and at peace with the world.

She was still undecided how firm she was going to be about not seeing Rafael again, but it was going to be difficult to avoid seeing him now that he was here, and she watched Doña Teresa's normally gentle face when she saw him.

Dorcas did not remember ever seeing Doña Teresa wear a frown before, but it was plain that she disapproved of Rafael being there, even though he had come no further than the gates of the *patio*. She left Dorcas's side and walked across to the gates, her head held high and her hands in a tight clasp in front of her, as disapproving as if he had presented himself at the gates of a convent, while Dorcas herself stayed in the background.

A small pale figure in a long, light-coloured dress, she stood beside the fountain, watching as he faced Doña Teresa's reproach. He looked across at her and she felt a twinge of conscience when she met those dark eyes, for not following and perhaps buffeting him against the reprimand that was bound to come.

Doña Teresa spoke to him in Spanish, her gentle voice edged with an unfamiliar hardness that surprised Dorcas as it apparently did Rafael. He said little in his own defence, but looked very much as if he wanted to cry as he stood on the other side of the wrought iron bars, then he lifted his head and again looked across at Dorcas, one hand extended towards her in appeal.

'Dorcas,' he pleaded, 'will you not at least come and speak to me, *mi amar?*'

Not knowing what Doña Teresa had actually said to him, Dorcas wondered how harsh she had been, and she could no longer ignore the plea. She nodded slowly, then walked towards the gates, her eyes anxious, and Doña Teresa turned to face her.

Her usually friendly dark eyes were sharp with anger, so that Dorcas blinked with surprise, although she did not pause or halt her approach. 'Dorcas,' she said quietly, 'do not be foolish, *niña,* you know that this is wrong!'

'Oh, Tía Teresa, please!' She was appealing as much for herself as for Rafael, she realised, for she hated the idea of incurring the old lady's wrath, but she felt she must be fair to Rafael. 'I—I promised I'd see Rafael again,' she reminded her. 'I owe him that much, Tía Teresa, even if it's only for a few minutes.' She put her own hands over the tightly clasped ones of Doña Teresa. 'Please,' she pleaded softly. 'I won't be more than a few minutes —a few seconds,' she amended hastily when she saw another frown forming.

Doña Teresa stood for a moment, looking from one to the other, her uncertainty plain in her eyes, then she nodded, albeit unhappily. '*Muy bien,*' she said at last. 'But please do not do or say anything foolish, *pequeña.* Do nothing that will bring disgrace upon our family, upon your brother.'

'Oh no, of course I won't!' Dorcas smiled her thanks and her relief, for she was convinced she would have obeyed if Doña Teresa had forbidden the *tête-à-tête.*

They watched her walk away, a solitary figure in the bright moonlight, her back straight and disapproving, unhappy at having allowed herself to be persuaded. It was not until she was lost among the scented riot of the trees and shrubs that Dorcas turned back to Rafael and opened one of the gates.

In a moment he was reaching out for her, with his hands outstretched eagerly, his dark eyes glowing as much with triumph, she guessed ruefully, as with passion, and she began to have doubts already about the wisdom of the meeting.

His arms pulled her close, pressing her to the virile warmth of his body, anxious to impress her with his masculinity, to let her know how much she would be missing if she turned him away. He held her for a moment before he bent his head and kissed her, his mouth firm and eager, his hands pressing her ever closer.

It was only because she had so recently been the recipient of Julio Valdares' fierce and disturbing attentions that she did not respond as Rafael expected her to, and in the circumstances he was bound to remark on her lack of response. The first time he had kissed her it had left her breathless and a little dizzy, and he obviously disliked a less impressive reaction this time.

'*Qué pasa, enamorada?*' he asked huskily. 'Do I not please you?'

Dorcas glanced instinctively at the villa, half hidden by the gardens behind her, softly illuminated by the moonlight and the yellow glow from its windows. 'You'd have pleased me better by not coming here, Rafael,' she told him quietly. It was difficult for her to remember her promise to Doña Teresa when he was being so persuasive, but she must be firm. 'It—it's not right for you to come here in the circumstances.'

'Circumstances!' Rafael declared scornfully, his eyes glittering darkly in the moonlight. 'I have to see you again, *mi amar*! I cannot live without you —I swear it!'

Such extravagant claims were flatteringly good for her morale, Dorcas had to admit, but it made her uneasy to have them declared so fervently when Doña Teresa might still be within earshot. Also the thought of Señorita Elena Valdares hovered uneasily in the back of her mind and refused to be dismissed. The girl was very much in love with Rafael, if her uncle was to be believed.

It was quite easy to believe that much at least, but it was more difficult for her to decide whether the betrothal had been arranged simply at the whim of a doting uncle. Don Julio had claimed that both his niece and Rafael had requested the arrangement, but Rafael had denied it, and she was very undecided who to believe at the moment.

Rafael could be very appealing, and while Don Julio was not easy to dismiss from her mind, at least for the moment she was free of his overpowering personality. 'I—I wish you wouldn't make such exaggerated claims, Rafael,' she told him, trying to make the scolding sound lighthearted. 'Even if you weren't to see me again you'd survive perfectly well and you know it!'

'*Condenar!*' Rafael swore softly. 'What must I do to make you believe me?'

'Perhaps I don't want to believe you!' The words were spoken almost without thinking, and she immediately wondered how true they were. It would have made things so much easier if only he had not made that first declaration of love to her. She had always enjoyed his company, but the idea of his being passionately in love with her had never really entered her mind until then.

'Dorcas!' He was gazing at her in hurt disbelief, his dark eyes glowing reproachfully in the moonlight. 'How can you be so—cruel? *Qué he hecho, mi enamorada*—please tell me?'

'You haven't done anything, Rafael!' It was so much harder than Dorcas had expected and she felt a small chill of regret that she had remained instead of letting Doña Teresa send him away, but somehow those dark eyes were irresistibly appealing and she was not nearly hard-hearted enough. 'It just won't work,' she added softly. 'Please believe me, Rafael, it won't.'

Whatever he would have said in his own defence Dorcas was not destined to learn, for at that moment lights appeared on the private road behind him and they both turned sharply to see the cause. A car's headlights were easy enough to identify, but the driver of the car was the point that disturbed Dorcas, as it did Rafael, if his expression was anything to go by.

He turned back to her briefly and there was a look of uncertainty in his eyes. '*Quién es?*' he asked curiously, and she shook her head.

The car, a big gleaming grey Rolls-Royce, came

round the final bend in the road and slid smoothly to a halt with Rafael, being nearer, held inescapably in its headlights. His whispered curse as much as her own intuition gave Dorcas a clue to the driver's identity, and her heart lurched crazily when he stepped out on to the stony road, closing the door quietly behind him.

Tall and authoritative and quite unmistakable, Julio Valdares paused for a moment, looking at them as they stood trapped in the beam of his headlights, then he leaned into the car again and switched them off, leaving only smaller side lamps streaking through the moonlit night and picking out their figures like characters on a stage. He crossed the few intervening yards in long easy strides and inclined his head briefly in a formal bow.

His dark, arrogant features looked even more dusky in the strong shadows and there was an air of suppressed strength about him that Dorcas found disturbing to her senses. *'Buenos tardes, señorita!'* The words like the bow excluded Rafael from the greeting and Rafael noted the snub with a swift flush of anger.

'Buenos tardes, Señor Valdares,' Dorcas replied, and glanced uneasily at Rafael.

She prayed he wouldn't be provoked into behaving rashly and she found the ensuing silence quite nerve-racking, although heaven knew why she always allowed Julio Valdares to make her so nervous. In this instance, she realised, it was because she remembered all too clearly that incident in the old olive grove this morning.

'I came to enquire after your wellbeing, *señorita,*'

he said in that deep, quiet voice that could play such tricks on her senses. The dark eyes spared a brief and derisive glance for Rafael, then he shrugged lightly. 'I can see that my concern was unnecessary,' he added. *'Perdón, por favor!'*

'Oh, but I'm—I'm grateful for your concern!' Dorcas assured him breathlessly, while Rafael looked at her narrow-eyed, his anger mingled with curiosity.

'You are ill, Dorcas?' he asked. 'I did not know!'

Dorcas hesitated before answering him, glancing at Julio Valdares through her lashes. He was watching her steadily, waiting for her to explain, and probably wondering just how much she would say, she guessed. 'I—I had a little too much sun this morning, that's all,' she said, and smiled at Rafael reassuringly. 'I wasn't ill, just a bit dizzy for a while, but Señor Valdares came to my rescue.'

She had made it sound as unimportant as possible, but Rafael was no more fooled than Julio was. 'Ah!' he said, and managed to get a wealth of meaning into the one short word.

Dorcas looked at him anxiously, but before she could say anything at all, Julio spoke to him in Spanish. Short, soft-spoken words that could have been gentle but for their effect on Rafael. His good-looking face flushed darkly and he clenched his hands into tight fists, so that for a moment Dorcas feared he might hit out.

Then he shrugged suddenly, his hands spread wide in a gesture that was at once both resignation and submission, and Dorcas wondered what on earth could have been said. He was looking at her again and shaking his head as if he had little choice in what he was about to say. 'It seems I must leave you again, *mi amar*,' he told her, his voice cold and shaking with suppressed emotion. 'But we will meet again, *si*?'

Dorcas felt horribly unsure of herself. It was difficult to think clearly on the spur of the moment and in such circumstances, and yet there was so much she wanted to settle. She wanted to settle things between them once and for all, but with Julio Valdares standing there like a god in judgment she couldn't think properly.

Again she glanced at Julio, but found no encouragement in that shadowy dark face, so that she frowned anxiously as she looked again at Rafael, trying to find the right words. 'I—I don't know if I can, Rafael,' she said in a small, husky voice, and he frowned.

'But, Dorcas, it is such a very short time now to the Fiesta de San Julio and I had hoped——' It was certain that the look Julio gave him was the reason he stopped short, but he shrugged his shoulders defiantly.

'Señorita Dorcas cannot attend the Fiesta de San Julio with you,' Julio informed him quietly. 'Your duty lies in another direction!'

The reminder, so sure and adamant, kept Dorcas silent, but Rafael's dark eyes darted swiftly to her, and his dislike of the situation was plain on his face. He knew he had little choice but to ride with Elena Valdares, but his reluctance to do so was evident from the way he tightened his mouth.

'*Madre mia!*' he swore softly. 'I will choose for myself!'

'You have little choice, *amigo*,' Julio told him

adamantly. 'You will of course be taking your fiancée!'

It was obvious that Rafael saw further argument as useless and he subsided with no more than a shrug of his shoulders, while Dorcas, touched by his unwillingness, put a sympathetic hand on his arm in consolation. 'But of course you'll be taking Señorita Valdares,' she said softly. 'It's the custom, isn't it?'

'It is the custom for betrothed couples to ride together,' Rafael agreed bitterly, and his dark eyes glittered when he looked at Julio. 'But if a man is not betrothed——'

'As you are to Elena,' Julio interrupted softly, and Rafael turned on him angrily.

'At the moment, *señor!*' he said harshly, and Dorcas caught her breath.

Rafael was being rash, but it seemed Don Julio was more than capable of dealing with his outburst and he merely curled his mouth disdainfully and murmured something in Spanish which made Rafael stare at him for a moment in stunned silence. Then slowly, he shook his head, looking again at Dorcas, his eyes uncertain. 'I cannot believe this is so,' he said, and the tip of his tongue flicked nervously across dry lips. 'If there was someone—' He shook his head again slowly. 'You would have told me!'

Dorcas's heart was racing wildly as she looked up at Julio Valdares' shadowy dark face. She had no idea exactly what he had said in those softly spoken words, but it was plain enough from Rafael's reaction what they implied, and she was almost too stunned herself to deny that there was another man in her life.

'I—I don't know what Señor Valdares said to you, Rafael,' she told him, 'but of course I'm not—I'm not serious about anyone—I'm not even thinking of it!'

'Ah!' Rafael breathed his satisfaction, and he reached for her hand and squeezed it. 'I knew it was so!'

'Whether or not Señorita Dorcas is engaged to be married,' Julio reminded him quietly, 'the fact remains, *mi amigo*, that you are. Elena, I know, is looking forward to joining the parade with you and I know that you will not disappoint her.'

It seemed to Dorcas that Rafael had more than met his match in Julio Valdares, and her heart pitied him. Rafael must surely have something of a conscience about Elena Valdares for the way he had been behaving lately, but he had no hope at all of outfacing her uncle, as Dorcas knew to her cost. He was in the wrong, but that would scarcely be an easy thing to admit in the circumstances.

For a moment Rafael merely looked at his antagonist in gloomy silence, then he shrugged, a heavy, despairing shrug that admitted defeat, and turned again to Dorcas. 'If I may see you, *mi hermosa*,' he said softly, but Dorcas was all too aware of the other dark eyes that watched her, and she looked down at her hands.

'I—I don't know, Rafael,' she said in a small, uncertain voice.

'Dorcas! *Por favor!*'

The plea was almost irresistible, but before she could do anything at all about it, she was aware that someone else had joined them, and she half turned to see Doña Teresa. She had presumably returned to see that Dorcas had carried out her promise to be no more than a few minutes talking to Rafael, and it was obvious that the sight of Julio Valdares surprised her.

Her momentary astonishment was banished by a welcoming smile, and she extended her hand in greeting. '*Buenos tardes*, Señor Valdares,' she said in her soft voice. '*Pase, por favor!*' She turned to Dorcas, gently scolding. 'Why do you keep Señor Valdares outside our gates, Dorcas?'

'I was enquiring after the *señorita*'s health, *señora*,' Julio informed her quietly before Dorcas could explain. 'I am pleased to learn that there are no ill effects after her—experience.'

That brief hesitation could have been significant only to Dorcas herself, but she felt the colour warm her cheeks as she glanced at both Doña Teresa and Rafael in turn. Rafael, however, was too troubled about his inevitable dismissal now that her aunt had arrived, and Doña Teresa apparently noticed nothing significant in it. She was smiling again at Julio, inviting him to enter.

'*Gracias, señora.*' He inclined his dark head in thanks, but he did not immediately avail himself of the invitation, instead he indicated with one hand that she should precede him, and Dorcas, horribly unsure of her next move, glanced uneasily at Doña Teresa.

'We would like you to join us again, *niña*,' Doña Teresa told her gently, and looked meaningly at Rafael who still hovered in the background. His good-looking features acquired a certain ageing strength in the beam of light that held him relentlessly in its glare and he looked dark and broodingly unhappy.

'*Adios*, Señor Montez,' she said firmly.

There was a finality about the words that struck Dorcas as incredibly cruel, especially coming from such a gentle soul as she had always thought Doña Teresa to be. It was almost as if the presence of Julio Valdares had inspired her, and Dorcas could see that he fully approved of Rafael's dismissal. But she couldn't be so heartless as to simply go in as she had been advised, leaving him there without another word and she turned impulsively towards him again and put a consoling hand on his arm.

'*Hasta la vista*, Rafael,' she said softly, and gasped when he snatched at her fingers, crushing them in his own and raising them to his lips.

'*Si, si, enamorada!*' he whispered hoarsely. '*Por favor!*'

The promise to see him again had perhaps been rash, but she had spoken impulsively and from the heart, trying in some way to compensate for the snub he had received. It was too late to go back now, but it was obvious that Julio Valdares would see it as yet another deliberate act of defiance, and somehow she regretted that more than she cared to admit.

'Dorcas!'

Doña Teresa's gentle voice held a hint of warning, and Julio was still standing close beside her, waiting for her to precede him through the gate, so she had little choice but to go. With an encouraging smile for the unwelcome visitor she turned and slipped past Julio, and as she did so her bare arm brushed against his scarred right hand, making her shy away swiftly as if she had been burned by the contact.

Glancing up, she caught the dark eyes looking at her with a strangely uncharacteristic glint of amusement in their depths and once again the colour flooded swiftly into her cheeks. Heaven knew what amused him, but she found herself remembering the savage fierceness of his mouth on hers, only hours before, and the idea of his possibly finding that amusing gave her a cold, curling sensation in her stomach.

As she walked back across the *patio* with Doña Teresa and Julio Valdares on either side of her, she felt suddenly rather like a runaway being brought back, and she shivered as she changed a brief backward glance over her shoulder.

Rafael was already gone, and the beam of the headlight showed only shrubs and trees and the bars of the iron gates in its path. The sound of a car being driven much too fast down the private road was diminishing rapidly and she knew that Rafael would be churning wildly with emotions as he drove. As uncertain as she was herself just what their future was.

'You are chilled, *señorita*?' The soft-voiced enquiry, only inches from her left ear, made her start and she she shook her head hastily.

'No, no, not at all!' she denied, although there were tiny shivers trickling along her spine as once more her arm came into contact with his hand, and he nodded.

'*Bien!*' he said softly.

'It's been such a long time!' Dorcas said, and for the hundredth time glanced at her wristwatch.

94

'What can they be talking about all this time, Tía Teresa?'

Doña Teresa shrugged her elegant shoulders and smiled, tolerant of her impatience without sharing it. 'Who can tell what things men discuss when they speak together?' she said in her soft voice, and Dorcas frowned impatiently.

'I'm surprised Ramón speaks to him at all,' she said bluntly. 'Not when he's been trying for years to acquire Casa de las Rosas by fair means or foul!'

Taking the adage literally, as she often did, Doña Teresa frowned. 'I do not think Ramón is such a *loco* as to submit to threats, *niña*,' she said quietly. 'You do Señor Valdares an injustice, I think, and your brother also!'

'Oh, I didn't quite mean it like that,' Dorcas denied hastily, 'but he'll do almost anything to acquire Ramón's estate, and I'm only glad that Ramón realises it!'

With the patient resignation of Spanish women, Doña Teresa shrugged her shoulders. '*Claro!*' she said quietly.

There were voices in the hall only seconds later and Ramón came in in his wheelchair, his visitor resting one guiding hand on its back without actually pushing it. In the brightly lit *salón* Dorcas found it even harder to meet those dark eyes as they sought hers across the room, and she kept her gaze on her brother, smiling a welcome.

'I was beginning to think you'd deserted us!' she told him, and laughed.

'I apologise, *señora, señorita*,' Julio Valdares said before Ramón could speak. 'The fault was mine.'

Ramón rolled his chair close to where Dorcas sat

95

on the wide, old-fashioned settee and took one of her hands in his, smiling at her as if he guessed how disturbed she was by the visitor. His long fingers played gently with hers and he spoke, as he often did, as if she was much younger than her twenty-one years.

'Don Julio was asking if you would care to learn to ride, *pequeña*,' he said, and laughed softly as he shook his head. 'I told him that I did not think you were very much disposed towards riding horses— you prefer the comfort of *el coche, no es verdad?*'

Struck dumb by the unexpectedness of it, Dorcas simply stared for a moment, then she chanced a direct look at the man who now sat beside her on the settee. 'I—I've never ridden a horse in my life,' she said in a small voice. 'And I've never really wanted to—thank you just the same, Señor Valdares.'

He shrugged his broad shoulders, as if her answer was no more than he had expected, and a hint of smile touched his wide mouth as he looked at her. 'It was merely a thought, *señorita*,' he said quietly. 'I have seen you admire the animals I ride, and I thought perhaps——' Again he shrugged. 'It is of no importance.'

His being there beside her on the settee gave Dorcas a disturbing sense of excitement and she did her best to still the wildly erratic beating of her heart and the curl of anticipation in her stomach. If only she was not so susceptible to that blatantly sensual masculinity he exuded she could act more naturally.

She wondered if he really had expected her to accept the offer to learn to ride, or if he had had some more devious motive for making the offer. She still could not bring herself to trust him, any more than she could resist his particular brand of mature sex appeal.

The dark eyes were watching her still, and she clasped her hands together tightly to resist looking at him again. 'Perhaps,' he suggested softly, 'you would care to visit the stables and *see* the horses? My mother would, of course, be present, and I am sure you would find it of interest, *señorita*.'

Feeling rather as if she had been trapped, Dorcas looked at Ramón, but saw only approval for the idea on his dark, strong face. For a moment her fancy saw him as cast much more in the same mould as Julio Valdares than as her own half-brother, and she blinked uncertainly before licking her lips.

'The—the horses are very beautiful,' she said at last in a small, uncertain voice. 'Perhaps—some time, *señor*, thank you.'

'Some time!' He echoed her words softly, and smiled, and she was once again stunned by the transformation it caused. His eyes crinkled at their corners and made a thousand tiny lines that went deep into the dark skin, and the eyes themselves glittered like jet between short, thick black lashes. There was a rakish, piratical look about the wide mouth and strong white teeth that gleamed in the dusky features and Dorcas's heart lurched violently in her breast as she curled her fingers into her palms.

He leaned forward slightly in his seat on the other end of the settee and spoke softly, almost intimately. 'I shall await your pleasure, *señorita*,' he told her with a hint of mockery. 'I hope I do not have to wait too long!'

He turned back to Ramón then, as if the subject was closed and of no further interest to him, and for a second or two Dorcas felt curiously bereft. So far Ramón had not indulged in his customary habit of smoking the long black Spanish cheroots he favoured, but he was too much of an addict to abstain for too long and murmuring an apology to his visitor he took one from the long box on the table beside him.

Apparently Julio Valdares did not smoke, for he not only refused to join his host, but looked at him in a curiously tense way as he took matches from the table. His eyes followed every move that Ramón made and for a moment Dorcas was puzzled by it. It was a minor and quite commonplace accident that gave her the answer, and she found it difficult to believe even when she saw it with her own eyes.

As he often did while lighting a cheroot, Ramón kept the match burning too long and dropped it hastily on to the big brass tray that formed the table top. It flared briefly, then died, but in those few seconds Dorcas saw the expression on Julio's face.

The wide mouth tightened, the lips drawn back in fear and the scarred right hand that lay on his knee curled into a tight fist as he stared at the sputtering flame on the brass tray with blank, dark eyes. Julio Valdares, she realised with a shock, still had a fear of fire.

CHAPTER SIX

IT was the following day that a small package was delivered to Casa de las Rosas, and Dorcas frowned curiously when it was first handed to her. She was sitting alone on the *patio* when Mercedes brought it to her, and a preliminary exploration with her fingers among the shrouding tissue gave her a clue to what it was. The realisation brought a swift disturbing flutter to her pulses and she looked up at the maid curiously, wondering if the messenger was still there.

'Did someone from Las Furias bring this?' she asked, and Mercedes nodded.

'*Si, señorita,* the servant of Don Julio.'

From her manner it was obvious that she was curious to know what gift was being sent to her employer's sister by their wealthy neighbour, but Dorcas had no intention of helping to satisfy her curiosity. She slid her finger-tips over the betraying smoothness of china among the enfolding tissue and had no need to guess that it was the substitute Saint Teresa they had argued about. Julio Valdares must always have his way, sooner or later, she thought ruefully, and smiled as she shook her head.

'All right, Mercedes, thank you!' She dismissed the maid before she attempted to open the box more fully, and she knew that by now Mercedes' curiosity would know no bounds.

The feel of the figure might have been similar through the concealing tissue, but once it was exposed there was absolutely no comparison between the little pottery statue she had dropped and broken, and the exquisite porcelain replica she now held in her hands. It was a work of art and must have been worth easily ten times the cost of the broken one.

For several moments Dorcas sat gazing at it, enchanted by its beauty and workmanship, but disturbed to think of Julio Valdares giving it to her so casually. Much as she was tempted to keep it and give it to Doña Teresa on her saint's day, she couldn't possibly accept such a valuable substitute, and she must tell him so.

She would not simply send it back, which could be taken for rudeness by a manners-conscious Spaniard, but return it personally and try to explain her reasons for refusing to keep it. It was when she went to replace the figure in its box that she discovered an accompanying note, and her heart was beating breathlessly fast as she unfolded the stiff cream paper and read it.

'*Señorita Dorcas*,' she read in a bold black script that somehow seemed to typify the man himself. '*Accept this San Teresa, por favor, in place of the one broken*'. It was signed simply—'*Julio Valdares*'.

Somehow the accompanying note made it more difficult to stick to her decision, but the figure was much too valuable to be casually given away by one stranger to another, and that was how she told herself she saw their relationship. She must be firm with herself, no matter how tempted she was. It might have helped to strengthen her resolve if she could have talked it over with Doña Teresa, but she still hoped to replace the gift with a similar one and she wanted it to remain a surprise.

Ramón was unavailable too, for she never disturbed him at this time of day unless it was absolutely necessary since he would be busy at his desk. So the decision of what to do with the Saint Teresa must be hers alone, and she was convinced it was the right one. She would drive out to Las Furias and return it personally and explain to Julio Valdares why she had to do so.

She found Doña Teresa in the *salón* and explained merely that she was going out for a while, without actually naming her destination. It was taken for granted that she was going shopping, as she sometimes did by taxi, so little comment was made on her going off alone.

The one who seemed most surprised by her destination was the taxi driver, a man who had taken her into San Julio several times. He looked puzzled when she asked to be driven to Las Furias, and glanced behind her, wondering if she was to be accompanied by Doña Teresa, no doubt, then repeated her destination to himself, as if to confirm it. 'Las Furias, *señorita*?' he asked, and Dorcas nodded.

'Yes, please.'

A brief but expressive shrug of his shoulders was his only comment, then he closed the door after her and climbed into his own seat. '*Muy bien, señorita!*'

Had she been travelling the same distance in England Dorcas told herself she would have walked, but it was much too hot to tackle the hill road and she had no desire to arrive looking dusty and dishevelled, also she felt it would give a more formal air to arrive by taxi. She had met none of the household, except Don Julio himself, and a hot and dusty stranger arriving on the doorstep was unlikely to be viewed with much favour.

When the taxi turned off the public road and on to the private approach to Las Furias Dorcas knew she had been wise not to try and walk, for it must have been easily half a mile along the tree-lined avenue to the villa, and much further than she had expected.

Tall plane trees shaded the wide approach road, merged here and there with eucalyptus and acacia, and their closeness to each other gave very little sight of the rest of the property. The villa itself, as they approached it, gave Dorcas another twinge of doubt, for it looked enormous behind its *patio* walls, sprawling luxuriously among such a riot of flowers and shrubs that she could scarcely believe her eyes.

Outside the walls of the *patio* wisteria and bougainvillea ran riot, hanging in great clusters from the walls, with hibiscus, poinsettias and deep red oleanders growing lower down, and even some homely hollyhocks sending their long spikes upwards to the bright Spanish sun.

Through the gates of the *patio* she could see even more luxuriant growth, with the same species that grew outside the walls covering the inside as well, along with roses and magnolias, tall palms and orange and lemon trees. Two huge fountains splashed into massive stone basins ornamented with dolphins and little naked stone boys squatting patiently on rocks, as if they waited for fish to appear.

'*Cuánto tiempo queda usted, señorita?*' the driver asked politely as Dorcas hesitated, looking through the tall wrought-iron gates that guarded the *patio*. 'Do you wish that I call back for you?'

Dorcas nodded vaguely, her courage almost failing now that she was there. 'I—I think so, please,' she said. 'In about——' She took time to consider how long it might take her to convince Julio Valdares that she could not possibly accept the Saint Teresa, and decided there was no possible way of anticipating it. 'Perhaps in about half an hour,' she decided at last, and the man nodded.

'*Media hora, sí señorita!*' He climbed back into his cab again and turned to look at her standing beside the big gates, his expression kindly but curious.

'You are not expected, *señorita?*' he suggested shrewdly, and Dorcas nodded. 'Ah!' A Spaniard could inject so much meaning into that one syllable and the driver nodded his head to indicate a black metal chain beside the gates. 'If the *señorita* sounds *la campana*, huh?'

Dorcas hesitated, then grabbed the chain and gave it a hard tug, resulting in a loud clanging above her head that startled her into gasping aloud, much to the driver's amusement. '*Bien!*' he applauded, and started up his engine again. 'O.K., señorita?'

The wide grin was somehow encouraging and Dorcas waved a hand gratefully. 'O.K.,' she agreed with a smile. '*Muchas gracias, señor!*'

'*Hasta luego, señorita!*' he called cheerfully as he started off down the long avenue. '*Adios!*'

The summoning bell was answered almost immediately, and Dorcas came under the scrutiny of a pair of suspicious dark eyes. A woman servant, she guessed, and not impressed to find a visitor at the gates with no visible means of transport. Dorcas smiled uncertainly, hoping the woman spoke English, for her errand would not be easy to explain in her own limited Spanish.

'Señor Valdares?' she enquired. 'Is he—is it possible for me to see Señor Julio Valdares, *por favor*?'

'The *señorita* is expected?' The question sounded cool and suspicious, but at least it was asked in very passable English, and Dorcas breathed a sigh of relief.

'No, no, I'm not expected,' she admitted with a wary smile. 'But I'm sure Señor Valdares will see me if you tell him I'm here, *señora*!'

For a moment the woman looked at her, undecided, still suspicious and definitely not enamoured of the idea of admitting a stranger merely on her own assurance. But before she could refuse outright, another figure appeared behind her, and as soon as Dorcas set eyes on the new arrival she knew in her heart that she was looking at Elena Valdares.

She was a girl about her own age, with short black hair and the same dark eyes as her uncle, but her skin was more golden than dusky and she was plumply pretty. She came to the gates and for a moment Dorcas again experienced the sensation of being weighed up, then the girl signalled to the woman to open the gate.

'Señorita James?' she enquired in a soft voice as she invited Dorcas to come in, and Dorcas nodded.

Meeting Elena Valdares had been a distinct possibility in the circumstances, but she had not known quite what to expect in the way of a welcome. So far there seemed less animosity than curiosity in her attitude, and at least the gate had not been barred to her. Dorcas extended a tentative hand which, after a brief hesitation, the other girl took in a rather limp gesture.

'You must be Señorita Elena Valdares,' Dorcas ventured.

A slight inclination of the dark head indicated a correct guess, but there was no accompanying smile and Dorcas felt embarrassingly uneasy. 'You wished to see my uncle, *señorita*?' Elena Valdares asked, and Dorcas nodded.

'If it's possible, *señorita*, please!'

The dark eyes studied her for a moment longer and they scarcely suggested encouragement. 'Don Julio is not expecting you?'

'No, he isn't,' Dorcas admitted. 'But I think if——'

'Oh, I am sure that he will see you, *señorita*,' Elena Valdares assured her in a cool voice, and managed to put a great deal of meaning into the answer so that Dorcas felt a warm tinge of colour in her cheeks.

'I wouldn't trouble Señor Valdares personally,' she explained, as if explanations were required, 'except that there's something I have to return to him and—and I feel I ought to explain *why* I'm returning it.'

'The Santa Teresa?' Elena asked, and a hint of

105

mischief lent a new suggestion of warmth to her features when she noted Dorcas's look of surprise. 'I saw my uncle remove the Santa Teresa from his collection,' she explained. 'I was curious enough to question his parting with one of his precious figures, *señorita*, and my uncle was honest enough to tell me his reasons and for whom it was meant.'

'Oh, I see.' Apparently Elena Valdares and her uncle were on very close terms, and somehow the realisation made Dorcas more uneasy than ever. 'Then—then you'll understand why I couldn't possibly take such a valuable piece as a replacement,' she said. 'It wouldn't be right—the one that was broken was no more than an inexpensive pottery figure, for all it was very attractive, but this one——'

'Is a rather valuable antique,' Elena said quietly, and confirmed Dorcas's suspicions. Elena smiled again, this time much more warmly. 'But I cannot think why you should wish to refuse the gift, *señorita*, surely in the circumstances——' Plump expressive shoulders lent a wealth of meaning to unspoken words and Dorcas stared at her for a moment, her eyes puzzled. There was no time to question the meaning, however, for light cool fingertips guided her across, through the lush cool of the *patio* with an air of determination that confirmed her as a Valdares. 'My uncle is with *los caballos*,' she said. 'I will have one of the servants ask him to come to the house, *señorita*.'

'Oh no, please don't do that!' Dorcas's heart thudded hard at her ribs when she thought of what Don Julio would do and say if he was interrupted at something important for no better reason than

106

to have her return the Saint Teresa he had sent her.

'But, *señorita*!' Elena looked at her curiously for a moment. 'It will be no trouble for someone to fetch my uncle and tell him you wish to see him.'

'But if he's busy——' Dorcas bit her lip.

'He will come,' Elena said with a certainty that Dorcas found discomfiting, and indicated a white iron seat beneath the spreading shade of a huge magnolia. 'Perhaps you would prefer to sit on the *patio*, *señorita*,' she suggested. 'I understand from my uncle that you enjoy to be outside in the air.'

'Yes, yes, I do.' It seemed strange that this girl knew so much about her, that Don Julio had spoken so much of her, and it was somehow oddly disturbing too.

Elena's plump hand indicated the garden seat. 'Then sit here in the shade, *señorita*,' she said, 'and I will send for my uncle to come.'

There could be no arguing with such determination, and Dorcas could only wonder that Rafael had managed to behave as he had been when he was betrothed to this strong-willed girl. The *patio* was cool and heady with a hundred scents and colours, briefly a haven until Don Julio appeared, and Dorcas sat on the very edge of the white seat waiting, while Elena sent one of the servants for their employer.

She returned after a few minutes and sat beside Dorcas, her hands in her lap, relaxed and at ease, in direct contrast to her guest's nervousness. Her pretty face smiled, but the look in her dark eyes was serious when she spoke, making the simple words she used sound so meaningful that Dorcas had no doubt she knew all about Rafael.

'You—you have met Rafael Montez, *mi novio*?' she asked in her perfect English, and Dorcas felt her heart begin a rapid, warning beat at her side.

Now that he had been mentioned, it was obvious that the subject of Rafael must have been on both their minds from the beginning, but it was not easy for Dorcas to talk about it, and Elena seemed bent on doing just that.

'Señorita Valdares,' Dorcas began, 'it—it's not easy to begin to say what I have to say, but——'

One soft cool hand on her arm stayed her in mid-sentence and Elena was shaking her head, a small and bitter smile on her mouth. 'I know that Rafael has been—escorting you, *señorita*,' she said, and Dorcas was stunned by her quiet self-control. Unless of course she was very adept at concealing her real feelings.

'But that's all,' Dorcas assured her hastily. 'We have driven about the countryside, looking at things that visitors always look at—no more.'

Whether she was convinced or not, Dorcas had no way of knowing, but briefly a small frown flicked across Elena's smooth features and her dark eyes were shaded by lowered lids, making correct assumption impossible. 'I have seen little of him these past weeks,' she said. 'It has been a—a difficult time for me.'

'Señorita Valdares!' Dorcas put a hand impulsively on the other girl's arm, and her eyes were anxious as she tried to convey the sincerity of what she was saying. 'Please—please believe that I didn't even know you existed until a few days ago,' she begged. 'If I had I would never have gone with

Rafael at all.'

'And since you have learned of my existence?' The question was quietly asked, but edged with harshness, and Dorcas sought to explain the hardest part of all.

'I—I admit I was reluctant to end my friendship with Rafael,' she said slowly at last. 'You see—you see he told me that your betrothal was—arranged and that he was an unwilling partner—I'm sorry!' she added breathlessly when she realised how that could hurt.

'Our betrothal was arranged,' Elena agreed, 'and Rafael consented to it, although whether it was because he truly wished to marry me or simply to please his family, I have never really known. I have preferred to think that it was because he wished to marry me—until you came, Señorita James.'

'I'm sorry!'

Again words failed her and Dorcas wondered at the irony of the situation. Until she came here she had seen Elena Valdares in her mind's eye as a spoiled and perhaps possessive girl who clung determinedly to an unwilling fiancé. Now that she had met her it was difficult not to like her and she could well understand Elena's uncle being so determined not to see her hurt.

Elena Valdares sat for a long moment, her hands in her lap, quiet and seemingly tranquil, although Dorcas knew that could not be so. Then she raised her head and looked at Dorcas with her dark eyes, a slight suggestion of tremor on her lower lip. 'Señorita James,' she said in her soft voice, 'if you would——'

Both heads turned in the direction of a sudden

sound from across the *patio*, the cause as yet unseen. The hard, clanging thud of an iron gate closing and a few seconds later the unmistakable tread of booted feet on the paved surface of the *patio*. There could be no doubt who the newcomer was and Dorcas had no idea whether or not Elena completed whatever request she was about to make, her heartbeat deafened her to everything but those approaching footsteps.

Julio Valdares came across the last few yards with a frown of curiosity on his face, his dark eyes searching Dorcas's features for a clue to her reason for being there. Elena had said he was with the horses and it was apparent that he had been doing some kind of manual work, for he was more informally dressed than she had ever seen him.

Fawn cord trousers tucked into long brown boots gave his muscular legs an even longer look and a rather stained fawn shirt was open almost to the waist. He had been working in the sun and he frankly looked as if he had, his dark face was beaded with perspiration which he brushed impatiently from his brow with a bare forearm and the shirt clung to his body damply.

His shirt being open as it was, nearly to his waist, it became evident that the small mark on his jaw that she knew to be the result of burns was only a small part of his injuries. A long, jagged blemish spread across half the broad chest, stark and vivid against the dusky smoothness of his skin. Yet despite the scars, or perhaps in part because of them, there was an earthy, primitive appeal about him that was infinitely disturbing, and Dorcas yet again despaired of her own vulnerability.

Elena smiled when he joined them and it was obvious that she had a great affection for her uncle, but Dorcas for her part, viewed his arrival with more apprehension. Close to he smelled tangily of horses and some spicy after-shave, the same tingling combination she had noticed before about him, especially when he had kissed her out there in the old olive grove.

'*Señorita!*' He inclined his black head briefly, and it was obvious that her presence there puzzled him for the moment. Then he flicked a glance at his niece and smiled ruefully. 'You did not say who it was required my presence, *pequeña*,' he said softly. 'You should have warned me that my visitor was Señorita James.'

'*Lo siento*, Tío Julio!' To Dorcas's sensitive ears the apology lacked conviction, and there was an oddly speculative look in Elena's dark eyes as she looked from her uncle to Dorcas.

Don Julio inclined his head again, this time as a gesture of apology for the informality of his dress. 'Your pardon, *señorita*,' he said in that deep, quiet voice. 'Had I known to expect your visit I would have been better prepared. As it is——'

'Oh, please don't apologise,' Dorcas begged hastily. 'I—I came on the spur of the moment, Señor Valdares, I don't expect you to receive me formally.'

Briefly the dark eyes swept the lush area of the *patio* for sign of a companion and seeing none he once more raised a querying brow. 'You came alone?' he enquired, and Dorcas nodded, realising for the first time just how easily such a call could be misinterpreted by the more formal Spanish mind.

'To see me?'

'I—I didn't stop to think,' she confessed. 'I suppose I should have in the circumstances—I'm sorry.'

'You have no need to apologise to me, *mi loca niña,*' Don Julio said. 'It is your own reputation that could suffer, not mine!'

'Oh, I don't think so,' Dorcas denied, though not very certainly. 'I—I could have come to see Señorita Elena, we're much the same age, and the taxi driver perhaps thinks I——' She shrugged, shaking her head. 'I don't think it matters,' she finished lamely.

'You are very careless with your reputation, *señorita,*' he declared softly but firmly, and Dorcas flushed. He was scolding her as if she was on a par with his niece and as much under his care, and she disliked the implication.

'You said yourself, *señor,*' she reminded him with studied calm, 'that I like to do things the English way.'

His dark eyes narrowed and he stood for a moment with his feet slightly apart, his big hands turned outwards and resting on his lean hips as he regarded her in silence. 'Since you have taken the trouble to call on me, *señorita,*' he said quietly at last, 'I assume you have some good reason. Do you wish Elena to remain while you tell me what it is you wish to see me about, or do you prefer the English way still?'

Aware that Elena was watching her with curious eyes, Dorcas shook her head, a faint pink flush betraying the fact that she knew he was mocking her and that it made no difference to her decision. 'I don't need a chaperone, Señor Valdares,' she told him. 'The few minutes I'll be here it isn't necessary to worry about my reputation!'

'*Muy bien, señorita!*' He regarded her steadily for several seconds and she bore the scrutiny uneasily, her fingers curling into her palms. It was quite maddening the way even a simple statement like that could affect her senses when it was accompanied by that dark-eyed scrutiny. Then he turned again to his niece, a hint of smile on his mouth that did nothing to assure Dorcas at all. 'As your services as *dueña* are not required, Elena,' he told her, 'you are free to leave us.' He added something in Spanish and Elena stared.

'But, Tío Julio——' A large hand silenced her protest and Elena shrugged resignedly, probably fully aware of the futility of arguing with him. '*Muy bien,*' she murmured, and gave Dorcas a small, curious smile that spoke volumes. '*Adios, señorita,*' she said softly. 'I am pleased that we have met.'

Dorcas took the proffered hand and smiled. 'I'm glad we have too, Señorita Valdares,' she said. 'Perhaps——' She glanced briefly at the towering figure of Don Julio beside her. 'Perhaps we could meet again.'

'Perhaps!' There was a brief, uneasy silence, as if Elena Valdares had something to say but found it too difficult to put into the words of a foreign language. Then she inclined her head politely in the traditional formal bow and turned back along the path to the house.

'*Señorita?*' The soft-voiced enquiry brought Dorcas back to earth and she looked up briefly to find those dark eyes watching her again, steadily and with a hint of speculation in their depths. 'Last night I invited you to visit Las Furias and look at the horses,' Don Julio reminded her quietly. 'Is it for this purpose that you are here, *niña*?'

'No—no, it isn't for that,' she denied, and would have explained her true reason for being there, but she was given no opportunity.

One large hand turned her to face the opposite way, the long strong fingers urging her forward, curled with irresistible strength round her arm. 'But now that you *are* here, *mi pequeña*, you will come and admire my horses, *sí*?' He asked the question in a voice that defied resistance and Dorcas did not even object to the free use of those evocative endearments.

She felt horribly and nervously undecided, but she suddenly realised that she was nodding her head in agreement, and her heart skipped crazily when he smiled. The *patio* gave access, via another wrought-iron gate, to the open parkland that she could see from her bedroom window, and she could realise how much more lush and beautiful it was to be actually walking in it.

Clusters of trees, mostly eucalyptus, spread down the entire slope of the hill towards the sprawling white stable buildings, half hidden by the massive shade of those umbrella-shaped fig trees. The hand under her arm held her within touching distance of the sensual warmth of his body through the thin skirt, and she found it infinitely disturbing, the whole experience was like something out of a dream and she realised with sudden clarity just where her impulsive determination to return the figure of the saint had led her.

'Señor Valdares.' She glanced up at him briefly, trying to find the right words to explain. 'I came to see you because——'

'You felt compelled to return the *figura*,' he suggested quietly, and a hint of smile again touched the corner of his mouth when she looked startled by the accuracy of his guess.

'You—you knew!' she accused, and he smiled again, shaking his head.

'Not until this moment,' he confessed. 'I could not think why it was that you were here, and then I remembered that I sent the *figura* by one of the servants this morning and I realised. I should have expected you,' he added with another smile.

In the shadow of the overhead trees his face had an even darker ruggedness and that lighter shading of scar tissue added to the suggestion of ruthlessness, so that Dorcas shivered involuntarily. 'You must see that I can't possibly keep anything as valuable as that,' she said firmly, trying to stop her voice from shaking. 'I insist on returning it, Señor Valdares!'

'Because it came from me?' They were right down near the boundary of the tree-shaded paddock now and he led her to the high, white wood fencing, resting one hand on the top bar as he turned to face her, a hard, black glitter in his eyes. 'Is that your reason, *señorita*?' he insisted harshly, and Dorcas shook her head.

'No! No, of course it isn't!'

'You lie, *niña*!' He faced her relentlessly, his one hand on top of the fence, the other still holding on to her arm and gripping her soft skin so tightly she bit her lip.

There seemed to be no one else about, although there must surely be grooms or stable-boys somewhere in the vicinity. Great piles of straw bales waited for someone to fork them into the open barns, and there was a big curved fork stuck into one of them as if someone had left off work only recently, and gone off somewhere. The air of desertion troubled her and she could not imagine why.

In the paddock several mares lifted their elegant heads and took a brief survey of the newcomers, then returned to their own interests, their soft movements the only sound except for the rustling of the fig trees overhead in the light warm wind. It was like a different world with no other inhabitants but herself and Julio Valdares, and that was a disturbing thought.

Determinedly keeping control of her voice, Dorcas looked around her. 'Where are all your men?' she asked, and Julio looked at her steadily for a moment without answering.

'It is the hour of luncheon,' he informed her then, in a quiet voice, and Dorcas looked up at him swiftly in startled disbelief.

'But it's early,' she said, searching that dark, enigmatic face with anxious eyes. 'It's much too early to be lunch time, especially in Spain.'

For a moment he said nothing, then the fingers holding her arm eased their tight grip and instead began a slow stroking motion that sent little shivers of anticipation shuddering through her body like the touch of ice. Her heart was hammering wildly in her breast and she could not control the shaking of her legs, curling her hands to try and steady her senses.

'Why are you so concerned with the absence of my *caballerizos*?' Julio asked softly, and Dorcas licked her lips nervously.

The last time she had informed him that she did not trust him, he had been angry enough to kiss her with such violence she could still shudder at the memory of it. But the fact was that she found herself with the awful suspicion that he had somehow sent all his men away so that they would be alone, and the idea set her heart beating so hard she felt it must stop.

Then a hint of a smile touched his lips briefly as he looked down at her. 'You once told me, *niña*, that you did not trust me,' he reminded her. 'Is it still so?'

Dorcas managed to hold his gaze for a moment, alarmingly uncertain. 'I—I just wish I knew *why* they're not here,' she told him, and he shrugged his broad shoulders.

'You would have been the object of many speculative eyes, *pequeña*,' he explained. 'I had Elena telephone before we came down here—there is work for them elsewhere.'

'I see.'

He apparently thought her satisfied and turned to look at the mares in the paddock, his gaze both critical and proud as he studied the smooth, shiny creatures so elegant with their arched necks and slim legs. A man like Julio Valdares, Dorcas thought a little hazily, belonged with such beautiful, mettlesome creatures.

She recalled the mention of the coming fiesta of Saint Julio last night, and wondered if Don Julio himself took part in the parade of riders that was such a feature of these occasions. And if he did it would be interesting to know if he rode alone or if a lady shared his mount.

With her eyes on the grazing mares she sought an answer to both questions, although she told herself she was being not only inquisitive but provocative in view of the conversation last night, with Rafael. 'Do you take part in the parade, señor?' she asked. 'For the fiesta of Saint Julio?'

Again his mouth curved into a smile and showed those incredibly white teeth against his dark face. 'Si, pequeña,' he said. 'It is my saint's day, and everyone takes part who can ride.'

Dorcas turned and faced the paddock, both arms along the top bar, her chin resting for a moment on her arms, an odd flutter of anticipation in her breast as she watched the mares grazing. 'Rafael will be taking Elena,' she said in a small voice that was as casual as she could make it.

'Si—claro, she is his novia!'

Holding tightly to the bar of the fence, Dorcas steadied her hands and again spoke without looking at him. 'And—and you, Señor Valdares?' she asked in a small, husky voice. 'Who rides with you?'

It was a long time before he spoke, and Dorcas felt as if her legs were about to give way beneath her while she waited, her ears alert for the slightest inkling of movement. One large hand still rested on the top of the fence close to her own, and the fingers curled tighter for several seconds until the knuckles showed white.

'No one rides with me, niña,' he said at last. 'No one at all!'

'I see.'

She continued to watch the horses, but her heart was in turmoil and for no other reason than that his voice had a strangely lonely sound when he made the confession. Perhaps there was more in Don Julio's life than she had so far learned. A broken romance perhaps, or a woman who preferred someone else, although it was difficult to imagine any woman having the strength of will to leave a man like Julio Valdares. It struck her forcibly suddenly that she did not even know if there had ever been a Señora Valdares.

The thought coming so suddenly and startlingly into her mind she turned, almost without realising it and looked at him with wide, puzzled eyes. It was the first time she had even thought about his being married and she found herself disliking the idea more than she cared to admit, though she could not, at the moment, think why.

'*Niña?*' The dark eyes were looking at her with an unaccustomed gentleness and she shook her head hastily to dismiss the alarmingly strong emotions that spun chaotically through her brain suddenly.

'Don't—I wish you'd stop calling me child!' she said with defensive sharpness. 'I'm not Elena, and I hate being patronised!'

It was unforgivable of her to have shattered the present tranquillity between them with such abrupt rudeness, and Dorcas would have given much to take back the impulsive words, but it was too late. She could see that when she looked at the dark anger on his face, glittering in the black eyes, and flaring the nostrils of that haughty nose.

The hawkish features had never looked more menacing and he glowered down at her for a second in silence, 'I need no reminding that you are not a child, *po'loca*,' he told her in a harsh, cold voice. 'But you provoke me too far, yet again! If you insist on playing the *coqueta* then you must take the consequences!'

Before Dorcas could do more than raise a faint cry of protest, she was seized by those hard strong hands and pulled against the unyielding steeliness of his body, while his mouth took hers with such force that her head was pressed back against his fingers and her lips prised apart violently.

Her own hands first thudded protestingly against him, then slowly she uncurled the fingers and laid them lightly against the sensual warmth of the dusky gold skin in a stroking, smoothing action that brought a soft, moaning sound from him. She was lifted suddenly into his arms and carried over to the pile of straw bales, then gently laid down upon them.

'*Pichón, mi poco pichón!*' The endearments whispered against her ear and Dorcas turned her head when his mouth pressed to the softness of her neck and throat. Strong gentle hands pushed aside her dress and caressed her smooth shoulders, and his body pressed her into the prickling scratchiness of the straw bales, warm and firm and enveloping her in that tangy, masculine scent of horses and after-shave.

Her own response to the sudden urgent needs of her own body would have alarmed her if she had been capable of realising them, but she was too delirious with new and exciting sensations to know what was happening. It was therefore all the more startling when she was suddenly put at arm's length, still held by those same strong hands but free of the pressure of his body as he looked down at her with glittering eyes.

Dorcas looked up at him, seeing a different man, another facet of that complex and passionate nature, and instinctively she raised her arms to him. For a moment he looked down at her with those bright, deep-glowing eyes, then he turned swiftly away and got to his feet, standing over her, his chest rising and falling more rapidly than was normal.

It seemed like an eternity that he stood there, and Dorcas held the black gaze as she never had before, her heart beating with unmerciful hardness at her ribs. Then slowly she curled her legs round and sat on them, sitting up and hugging her knees, strangely bereft suddenly and oddly sad.

'I will return you to your brother,' he said quietly at last, and reached down with his hands to help her to her feet. There was barely a trace of unsteadiness in his voice and Dorcas, her own emotions in turmoil, wondered how he could appear so untouched by the incident. He stood with her hands in his for several seconds, then shook his head slowly. 'I must apologise,' he said, so formally that Dorcas shrank from her own turbulent reaction. 'I should not have allowed you to provoke me so far!'

Provoke him—so that was how he saw her objection to being called a child! She drew away her hands swiftly and curled them into tight fists at her side, then reached down and recovered her handbag where it had fallen in the straw, clutching it tightly in front of her. 'You don't have to take me home,' she told him in a voice she tried hard to control. 'I have a taxi coming for me.'

'Dorcas——' He reached out and would have touched her cheek with that disturbingly gentle touch again, but she drew back, unready to be subjected to another emotional assault so soon, and feeling much too much as if he saw her only as a child in need of reassurance.

She was vulnerable, she realised it only too well, where Julio Valdares was concerned, and his gentle, apologetic politeness was unbearable after those brief, wild moments just now. 'No!' She turned her head sharply, and bit back the tears that threatened. 'I don't need you to be sympathetic, or apologetic,' she told him in a breathlessly small voice. 'I just want to go!'

She was half turned when his hand reached out and touched her arm and she shook him off, snatching her arm away, free of those persuasive fingers. 'Dorcas, don't be foolish!'

'I never want to see you again,' she whispered shakily. 'Never!'

'But you cannot walk home, *po'loca*!' he called after her as she ran, but she paid no heed to his reasons. 'Dorcas, wait!'

With the fear in her mind that he might follow her she took to her heels and ran, not really knowing in which direction she should go, as long as it was away from him. The sun beat down on her relentlessly as she battled against the slope of the hill, but she still ran. If she was lucky she would not have to see either the woman servant or Elena Valdares again, and she would worry about the taxi driver when she was more able to think clearly.

Visiting Las Furias had been a mistake, and she would never go again under any circumstances. It did not yet occur to her that the little figure of Saint Teresa that had started it all still nestled in her handbag, still not returned to its owner.

CHAPTER SEVEN

'I AM at a loss to know why you should behave so—
so rashly, Dorcas,' Ramón said in his excellent but
pedantic English. 'Did you not realise the complications that could follow upon your paying a call
on a man in his own home, unaccompanied?'

After much heart-searching, Dorcas had decided
that it was probably best to tell Ramón about her
visit to Las Furias herself, for it was not beyond the
bounds of possiblity that he would hear of it from
Don Julio himself. She had so far told him no more
than the fact that she had called at the villa and
made no mention of her reasons for going or of
those last few shattering minutes alone with Julio
Valdares.

'I didn't even think about it being anything un-
toward,' she confessed, much as she had explained
to her host at Las Furias, and Ramón shook his
head despairingly.

'And suppose neither of the Valdares ladies had
been at home?' he asked. 'Would you have returned without seeing Don Julio himself?'

Dorcas took only a moment to think about it,
then she shook her head. 'I doubt it,' she admitted.
'I had to see him and—well, it seemed a perfectly
straightforward thing to do.'

Ramón looked up sharply, his eyes narrowed

suddenly. 'You *had* to see him, Dorcas? Why?'

She hesitated. Maybe Ramón would not see eye to eye with her on the necessity of returning that valuable little figure to its owner, for after all, Don Julio's own niece had seen no reason for her refusing to keep it. 'It's a long story,' she said, and Ramón frowned.

One long hand tapped the edge of the desk impatiently, as if he suspected she was withholding something, and Dorcas was reminded again how much alike her brother and Julio Valdares could seem on occasions. 'I would like to hear it, *por favor*,' Ramón told her quietly, and Dorcas sighed inwardly at the inevitable.

One thing she was learning about the Spanish male was his dogmatic insistence on being kept in the picture about everything that concerned his womenfolk. She could well imagine that, given a similar situation, Ramón would be as fiercely protective about her as Don Julio was about Elena— hence their seeing eye to eye on the matter of Rafael Montez.

She perched herself on the edge of Ramón's desk, one slim bare leg swinging as she talked, her fingers playing absently with an obsolete but beautiful silver inkstand. 'As you know,' she said, 'it's Saint Teresa's day soon, and I found a lovely little figure of her in a shop in San Julio that I wanted to give to Tía Teresa.'

'That was thoughtful of you, *niña*,' Ramón smiled, and Dorcas pulled a rueful face.

'Unfortunately,' she told him, 'I broke it as I came out of the shop. I suppose it was my fault, as he said, but——'

'He?' Ramón prompted, and she sighed.

'Don Julio Valdares, of course,' she said, as if she was resigned to the fact that Don Julio was responsible for everything that happened to her lately. 'He was coming past the shop as I came out,' she explained, 'and we literally bumped into one another. The little Saint Teresa fell to the pavement and was smashed to pieces—I could have cried!'

'And did you?' Ramón enquired softly. There was a gleam in his eyes as if he knew the answer well enough, and Dorcas shrugged.

'I might have shed a few tears,' she admitted reluctantly. 'But the point was that I blamed him for making me drop it and he insisted on replacing it with one of his own. He sent it over by one of the servants yesterday morning, but of course I couldn't possibly keep it.'

Ramón's reaction was very much the same as Elena Valdares' had been. He raised one brow and looked at her curiously. 'You refused to accept it?' he asked, and she nodded.

'I didn't exactly refuse to accept it,' she said. 'That is, I didn't simply send it back, I wanted to explain why I couldn't take it. It's a very valuable antique, for one thing. The one I bought for Tía Teresa was very nice, but it wasn't worth a fraction of the one he sent to replace it!'

Ramón was shaking his head and it was plain that he was not at all pleased. 'So, instead of consulting either Tía Teresa or me,' he said, 'you went running off to Las Furias to return it? Oh, Dorcas, could you not have been more—diplomatic?'

Dorcas swung her foot, watching the open toe of her shoe as it brushed back and forth against the

126

shiny wood desk. 'I'm not a diplomat, Ramón, you know that,' she said. 'I just knew I couldn't keep that figure, so I took a taxi and went out there to see him and explain *why* I couldn't keep it!'

'And you saw him?'

'I saw him,' Dorcas agreed, eyes downcast. Even now she could see that tall, toil-stained figure in her mind's eye, coming across the *patio* towards her, his dark eyes full of surprise when he saw her. 'The figure was part of a valuable collection,' she added, bringing herself sharply back to earth. 'So Señorita Elena told me.'

Ramón was eyeing her speculatively, and she felt as if her whole attitude towards Don Julio was under critical scrutiny. 'And yet he gave it to you,' he mused, and one long hand rubbed his chin thoughtfully. 'I might wonder why, *niña*, if I were a suspicious man!'

Dorcas felt the colour warm her cheeks and she slid from the edge of the desk to stand with her hands tightly curled, a hint of anger in her blue eyes as she looked down across the desk at him. 'If you think there's any reason—any reason at all, for him to give me expensive presents,' she said in a small tight voice, 'you're wrong, Ramón!'

Ramón leaned forward in his chair and reached for her hand, drawing her round the desk to stand beside him. He looked up at her curiously, his dark eyes searching for answers. 'Tell me what happened, *niña*,' he urged softly, and added before she could voice the denial that formed on her lips, 'and do not tell me that the visit was uneventful, for I know from your manner that it was not!'

Close to his face looked drawn and lined and it

was a temptation to reach out and touch the lines, try to ease them away. She loved Ramón perhaps more than a lot of sisters did their brothers, possibly because they had not been through the usual traumatic jealousies of youth together, and she valued his opinion of her more than she cared to admit. She would hate to do anything to hurt him or to lessen his good opinion.

'The woman servant wouldn't even let me in, until Elena Valdares came along,' she explained, after a moment or two. 'I—I liked her, Ramón, and I think she quite liked me, as much as she could in the circumstances. And then——' She hesitated, wondering how much she should make of the ensuing incident. 'Don Julio came and he took me to see the horses. He—he asked if I wanted Elena to come with us,' she explained earnestly, 'but—well, I saw no reason for her to, so I went with him alone.'

Ramón's head shook slowly, despairingly. 'Oh, Dorcas!'

'He asked her to phone ahead and have the men moved to other jobs before we got there,' Dorcas went on hastily. 'He said it was to save me embarrassment, and I believe that was his reason, Ramón, honestly.'

'I believe it too, niña,' he said quietly. 'But you were very foolish just the same. Don Julio is a man of some   ' An expressive Spanish shrug left no doubt of his meaning.

'He kissed me,' Dorcas said simply. 'That's all, Ramón.'

'That is all,' Ramón echoed softly, and shook his head. 'You are a foolish child, Dorcas, and it was fortunate for you that Don Julio is the man he is, or the consequences might have been very much more serious than one kiss. Do you realise that?'

'Of course I realise it!' sighed Dorcas. Remembering how willingly she had responded to that kiss, even now she felt her heart skip in a brief return of that blood-stirring excitement he had aroused in her. 'Well, it won't happen again, you can take my word for it!' she assured him. 'I've told him that I never want to see him again and I mean it! He's quite the most arrogant, annoying man I've ever met, and I don't care if he takes offence or not, I'm sending back that figure of Saint Teresa!'

'Dorcas——'

'I've made up my mind,' Dorcas insisted, freeing her hands and walking back round the desk to face him across its width. 'I'll pack it up and send it back!'

'No, *niña!*' His firmness made her stare at him in blank surprise for a moment, but there was no mistaking the determined gleam in Ramón's dark eyes, and he looked more stern than she had ever seen him look. 'This is a matter of—good manners,' he told her, more quietly. 'To return a gift offered in return for one that was broken would be unforgivably rude, Dorcas, and I cannot permit you to do such a thing for no better reason than your childish dislike of the donor.'

'Childish?' She repeated the accusation with distaste. It was all too reminiscent of the man they were discussing, that reference to her youth, and she hated to have Ramón see her in the same light as Julio Valdares.

'You have little reason for your dislike, *pequeña*,' Ramón insisted gently. 'The matter of my selling the Casa de las Rosas to him is the only reason you have taken such a dislike to him, is it not?'

'Isn't it enough?' Dorcas asked. She resented the fact that she was beginning to appear as the villain of the piece, while Don Julio Valdares was rapidly being cast as the injured innocent.

'I appreciate your concern for me, *niña*,' Ramón told her softly, 'but it is quite unnecessary, and I would much rather you saw in Don Julio the pleasantly charming man he is, instead of trying to make him the villain.'

Seeing him as the villain was, Dorcas had to admit, the only thing that kept her from seeing Julio Valdares as something much more disturbing. She was all too well aware of his charm and his other, more virile attractions—losing her one reason for disliking him would make her much too vulnerable, and she trembled at the very idea of that.

'You—like him, don't you?' she asked, and Ramón made a moue of admission, then smiled.

'I find him a pleasant and personable neighbour,' he said quietly. 'I have no reason to see him as anything else, *mi poco hermana*, have you?'

It took Dorcas several seconds to bring herself to the point of admitting it, then she shook her head slowly. 'I suppose not,' she said after a moment or two.

Having driven into San Julio to do some shopping, Dorcas had, almost inevitably, popped into the little church in the square to enjoy a quiet moment. San Julio looked down at her benignly from his carved stone niche, and she sighed as she studied him, envying his look of divine tranquillity. His namesake had been causing her a great deal of heart-searching lately, and he seemed to be on her mind far more often than she liked.

Meeting Elena Valdares had caused her a lot of unrest too, for she found it much harder to condone Rafael's behaviour. The meeting had been brief, it was true, but it had been long enough to convince Dorcas that the Spanish girl would be very deeply hurt if her betrothal to Rafael was ended. It had little to do with pride—Elena loved him deeply and the thought of causing her more unhappiness was something Dorcas faced unwillingly.

She had seen nothing of Rafael during the last couple of days, and Julio had appeared only as a distant figure on the skyline, further down the hill, tall and autocratic on one of his beautiful horses. She had not waited for him to appear again, among the boundary trees that bordered the neglected olive grove, as she always had, but turned back to the house each time, to avoid a meeting.

Their last encounter had been much too emotionally disturbing for her to be able to return simply to exchanging formal greetings as they had always done, and anything more intimate was out of the question while he saw her as no more than a young girl able to provoke him into occasional passionate outbursts that he soon regretted.

With a last envious glance at the placid stone saint, Dorcas made her way quietly from the church and out into the sunlit Plaza de San Julio again. Her shopping was done and she had several minutes until her taxi came for her, so she chose to wait for it in one of her favourite places. A long stone bench set under a cluster of shading palms offered a view of the passing scene and the cool sound of the fountains in the centre of the plaza.

Putting her shopping on to the seat beside her, she leaned back against the backing wall behind her, her eyes drooping sleepily and her mind wandering into the realms of speculation. She was jolted back to earth with startling suddenness by the clamour of motor horns and angry Spanish curses, all directed at the driver of a car which had suddenly swerved in towards the kerb and stopped immediately in front of her.

She recognised the car easily enough, and her heart began thudding anxiously when the driver leap out of his seat and ran across the few yards of paved walk to stand in front of her. Black eyes looked down at her, gleaming with pleasure at the sight of her, and Rafael reached down to take her hands in his, lifting them to his lips and murmuring words of Spanish which she could not understand, nor wished to hear at the present moment.

'Rafael!' She got to her feet and withdrew her hands from his grasp as firmly as she could without appearing to snatch them away. 'Please don't behave as if you haven't seen me for years—you embarrass me!'

'Oh, *mi enamorada*!' Rafael appealed in a throaty whisper. 'How can you treat me so? I am glad to see you and you look at me as if I was some stranger accosting you in the street! *Madre mía*, how cruel you are!'

Dorcas was horribly undecided what to do for the best. There was quite a lot she wanted to say to Rafael, but at any moment now her taxi would be arriving and she would be off. If Rafael offered to take her home instead, as he almost certainly would, it would simply prolong something that she knew ought to finish right here and now, but she had to explain to him about her meeting with Elena, and her own determination not to see him again.

'*Mia amar!*' Rafael said softly, trying to take her hands again. 'Will you not talk with me for a little while? I have not seen you for two whole days and I have missed you!'

'I—I can't come with you, Rafael.' She looked around the little *plaza* almost desperately. If only her taxi would come her problem would be solved. 'I'm expecting my taxi any minute now, and I really shouldn't be seen with you.'

'I will send the taxi away and drive you home myself,' he insisted, as she had known he would. 'Then we can talk, *verdad*?'

Dorcas shook her head, determined to be firm. It was a last ditch stand for what she now knew to be right. 'No, Rafael,' she said, 'I'd rather go by taxi! I—I'll write to you and explain—everything, I promise, but I'd much rather not arrive at Casa de las Rosas with you!'

'Write to me?' The idea had come to her on the spur of the moment and it was obvious that it stunned Rafael, for he was gazing at her in disbelief and shaking his head slowly. 'But you cannot mean this, Dorcas! This—this write to me, what is there to explain? Have you not considered this betrothal that keeps us apart? Have you not said that I have been forced into such an arrangement and that you will support me?'

'I've said nothing of the kind!' Dorcas denied hastily. She shook her fair head vehemently and her hands held the packages she had bought in tight, tense fingers as she looked up at him. 'I—I admit that I thought you might have been pushed into something you didn't want or properly understand, Rafael, but now——'

'Now?' Rafael prompted softly, and his eyes narrowed. 'How is it so different now, *pequeña*?'

Dorcas shook her head, looking down at her packages rather than at that dark, handsome face with its black eyes accusing her of treachery. 'I've met Elena Valdares,' she said quietly, and heard the sudden intake of his breath.

'So!' Like most of his race Rafael could put a wealth of meaning into one simple word, and it was not hard to guess that he saw Julio Valdares as the instigator of her meeting with Elena.

'I—I liked her, Rafael,' she told him, her voice not quite steady. 'She's very nice and she doesn't deserve to be hurt as you're hurting her.'

Anger glittered brightly in Rafael's black eyes now that he saw she was adamant, and he stood in front of her, blocking her way, his slim body taut with emotion and determined not to be brushed aside. 'And how did you meet Elena, *mi pequeña*?' he demanded. One hand encircled her right wrist with enough strength to make her wince and he peered closely into her face. 'Who brought you together, Dorcas? Agh!' He swore softly in his own tongue without giving her time to answer. 'I do not need to ask who wishes to drive a wedge between us for the sake of his precious *sobrina*! Don Julio Valdares!'

He spat out the names as if he hated every one of them, and Dorcas shrank from the fierceness of his passion as she tried to free her captive wrist without struggling too obviously. 'It wasn't Don Julio!' she denied breathlessly. 'He had nothing at all to do with it! And please, Rafael, let go my wrist, you're hurting me!'

It was evident that he wished to see only Don Julio as responsible for Dorcas's new determination to finish with him, but she was so obviously telling the truth that he was bound to believe her, however unwillingly, and he stared at her for a moment in silence.

'If he did not arrange this way to—to touch your conscience,' he asked in a low harsh voice, 'then who did?'

Dorcas was unwilling to admit that she had gone to Las Furias on her own with the express purpose of seeing Julio, but it was the only way of convincing Rafael that the meeting with Elena had been entirely her own doing. 'There—there was something I had to go to Las Furias for,' she began slowly and with obvious reluctance, and Rafael frowned at her suspiciously.

'You went to Las Furias?'

Dorcas nodded. 'I—I had to take something to Don Julio, and——'

'Take something to him?' Rafael eyed her suspiciously. 'For your brother, perhaps?'

'No, no, not for Ramón.' She frowned anxiously. It was something—something that Don Julio sent to me that I had to return. Nothing very important or personal, but I had to go and see him and explain why I couldn't keep it and so—I went to Las Furias to see him.'

Rafael, it was clear, found the explanation hard to believe and he stared at her in silence for a moment, then shook his head again slowly. 'You called upon him alone?' he asked at last, and Dorcas nodded. 'You called upon a man at his home without someone accompanying you?'

'I didn't think about it,' she confessed, 'until Don Julio reminded me how rash I'd been. It was Señorita Elena who admitted me.'

'Ah!' Again the single syllable spoke volumes, and Dorcas hoped the explanation would calm him down, allow her to leave him without fuss now that he knew about her meeting Elena.

'I liked her,' Dorcas said, anxious to impress him with her reasons for being so adamant about their parting. 'I don't like to see her hurt, Rafael, and she is going to be hurt, because she loves you so much.' His frown was more impatient than disbelieving, and Dorcas tried once more to impress upon him the impossibility of their continuing as they had been. 'When you ride with her behind you on the day of the fiesta it will be like the public announcement of your betrothal and there'll be no question of our being seen together again, so there's no point in going on!'

'Then I will not ride with her!' Rafael declared passionately. 'I will ride with you behind me, *enamorada*!'

'You will not!' She was more than ever desperate to convince him because she could see the taxi she had ordered coming across the *plaza* and she wanted to be able to leave him without too much exhibitionism. Her head was spinning with confusion and she sought for a way out without even stopping to think of the consequences. 'I'm riding with Julio Valdares!' she declared breathlessly, and Rafael's jaw dropped.

'*Madre de Dios!*' he breathed piously, and the grip on her wrist tightened rather than eased. 'He has no right!'

'He has more right than you have, Rafael,' Dorcas insisted, managing to keep her voice low only with conscious effort. 'Now will you please let go of my wrist,' she begged. 'Please, Rafael, my taxi's here and I have to go.'

'I will drive you!' He turned, ready to dismiss the approaching taxi, but Dorcas was shaking her head anxiously.

'No, Rafael, please!'

His fingers still encircled her wrist and he was looking at her with dark, glittering eyes, tightening his hold until she gasped in protest. 'I will send him away and you will come with me!' he insisted in a harsh, determined voice. 'We have much to say, Dorcas, *mi amar!*'

There were people all over the little *plaza*, plenty of whom would no doubt have come to her rescue had she made a scene, but she was reluctant to be involved in a public display of Latin temperament, which was bound to happen if she protested too vociferously. The taxi was approaching from her right and another car drew into the kerb from the left at the same time, so that the two vehicles stopped almost nose to nose, behind Rafael and out of his sight.

Too involved with avoiding a scene with Rafael, Dorcas paid little heed to the other car, but had eyes only for the taxi driver, and she frowned anxiously when a glance at his stationary cab revealed another flaw in her escape route. The driver of the other car was Julio Valdares and he was now striding purposefully across the pavement towards them, while the taxi driver beamingly thrust money into his pocket and shrugged with Latin appreciation of easy money.

'Julio!'

Dorcas stared at the newcomer in dismay, tugging frantically at her captive wrist, uncaring now whether her struggles created a scene or not, she simply had to get away. After what she had just told Rafael about riding with him in the fiesta parade, Julio was the last man she wanted to see.

She sped across the pavement in urgent haste, pursuing the departing taxi and leaving Rafael staring after her. Swerving to avoid Julio on the way, she waved an arm frantically at the taxi driver, but to no avail, but with only one hand to hold her packages one of them slipped from her grasp and fell to the ground.

There was a sickening crunch as it fell that she recognised as broken glass. A bottle of perfume she had bought now lay at her feet, its contents already seeping through the gaudy wrappings on to the sun-warmed pavement, and she could have wept. Not only had she lost her taxi but a bottle of her favourite perfume as well, and yet again Julio Valdares had been indirectly responsible for the catastrophe.

It took only a couple of his long strides to bring him to her side and a large hand was placed gently on her arm in consolation. '*Qué mala suerte!*' he said, and added, 'Am I also responsible for this—accident?' in such a soft, quiet voice that it was impossible for her to turn and berate him. 'You appear to be extremely unfortunate with your purchases, *pequeña!*'

Nothing could be done about the tears that trembled on her lashes when she looked up at him, and she had a sudden strange and inexplicable urge to be taken into his arms and comforted. That softly spoken endearment did nothing to help her self-control either.

'Why—why did you have to come?' she whispered huskily, and even through her tears she saw the smile that crooked the corner of his wide mouth and glowed for a moment in his eyes as he looked down at her.

'Were you willingly standing there with Rafael Montez?' he asked, and without answering Dorcas hastily lowered her eyes. 'I thought not!' he said softly.

Rafael hesitated only briefly, then he too came striding across to join them, and there was no doubt that he was even less pleased to see Julio Valdares than Dorcas was. His black eyes glittered resentment at the intrusion, and he stood the other side of her stiff and angry. 'Dorcas,' he said, pointedly ignoring her companion, 'may I help you?'

Dorcas shook her head. She was so close to weeping with sheer frustration and confusion that she dared not speak, and Julio took it upon himself to answer for her. 'The *señorita's* perfume is the

139

only casualty, *mi amigo*,' he informed the glowering Rafael calmly. 'And since the accident was almost certainly due to my appearance on the scene, I am sure that I shall be allowed to replace it without dispute.'

'Oh no, Señor——' She remembered suddenly a similar and futile argument concerning the figure of Saint Teresa, and hesitated against starting another. Another faint smile was enough to tell her that he too remembered and realised the reason for her hesitation.

'*Señor!*' Rafael was stiffly formal, and his black eyes glittered at the older man resentfully. 'You will excuse us if we leave,' he said, and thrust a possessive hand through the curve of her arm, drawing her close against him. 'I am driving Señorita James to her home. *Adios, señor!*'

Julio looked at him steadily for a second, then one large hand reached out and took Dorcas's right wrist in gentle fingers, turning it to show the angry red marks left by her unsuccessful efforts to free herself of Rafael's grip. 'And does the *señorita* go willingly with you, *amigo?*' he asked with dangerous quietness, and it was not only Dorcas who recognised the anger behind the soft-voiced question.

Rafael's good-looking face flushed as he looked at the marks, then he shook his head as if to deny responsibility for them, one hand running through his black hair. '*No es culpa mia*,' he said, but Julio was relentless and his dark eyes glittered while he held her bruised arm in gentle, strong fingers.

'Then whose fault, *amigo?*' he demanded coolly. 'Are you saying that the *señorita* is at fault for trying to free herself from you?' The dark eyes raked over him with such unmistakable scorn that even Dorcas flinched. 'How gallant you are, *señor*! I hope you are never so—persuasive with your *novia*, or you will almost certainly answer to me!'

Dorcas could scarcely believe it was happening, right there in the middle of San Julio, with people milling about them and in broad daylight. Remembering his own passionate violence it was difficult to concede him the right to be so contemptuous of Rafael, but there seemed little she could do and her heart was hammering with relentless force against her ribs. A small inexplicable curl of excitement was churning in her stomach too and making her head spin.

Julio had the whip hand and they all three knew it. 'If you will remove your hand from the *señorita's* arm,' he said with quiet confidence. 'I will see that she returns safely to her brother's house.'

Rafael's eyes narrowed, but he made one last attempt to stand his ground against that remorseless contempt. 'You do not have the right, *señor*,' he began, 'to——'

'As the uncle of your *novia* I have the right!' Julio said with chilling firmness, and Dorcas felt the fingers of Rafael's hand curl more tightly for a moment before they were withdrawn with reluctant slowness.

She could feel him trembling with the violence of his anger, but he knew when he was beaten and at last he gave a small, stiff bow by way of surrender, then reached for her hand and raised it to his lips. '*Lo siento*, Dorcas,' he said in a voice that was flat with anger. 'I hope—I *know* I will see you again!' His black eyes glanced malevolently at

Julio, and he tightened his mouth. 'Think with care about your decision to ride in the *fiesta, mi amar,*' he warned. 'Tradition is strict and to ride with——' he shrugged meaningly and Dorcas flushed, 'such a man is dangerous, *enamorada.*'

She foresaw almost unbearable embarrassment if the matter of her rash statement was raised here and now, and she shook her head urgently, aware that Julio was watching her narrow-eyed and curious. 'Please!' she whispered anxiously, and Rafael shrugged, then pressed his mouth fervently to her fingers again, in a gesture that was plainly defiant.

'*Adios, mi hermosa!*' he murmured, and turned and was gone before she could reply.

Watching him walk to his car, Dorcas could not help feeling pity for him in his defiance. Sooner or later he had to come to terms with the inevitable. Once he rode in public as Elena's official fiancé perhaps the problem would resolve itself; for both their sakes she hoped so.

'*Señorita?*'

The gentle prompting brought her back to earth and she glanced up into Julio Valdares' dark, autocratic face with a certain sense of anticipation. The curve of that wide, expressive mouth reminded her of their last disturbing encounter and she hastily looked away again.

She had been convinced that she meant what she said when she told him she never wanted to him again, but now that she was with him, she felt much less certain. Her heart was beating rapidly and the hint of possessiveness in the touch of his hand on her arm did strange things to her emotions. If he meant to offer to drive her home she was not at all sure that she would have the will to refuse.

'I—I wish you hadn't sent my taxi away,' she said in a small uncertain voice, and he raised a curious brow.

'Did you not mean to send him away and drive with Rafael Montez?' he asked, and Dorcas shook her head.

'No! No, I didn't! That's what I was trying to tell him when you came!'

'Ah!' His dark eyes gleamed for a moment as he ran them speculatively over her flushed face. 'So you *were* unwilling to go with him!' One brow questioned her and he smiled as he looked at her. 'And will you also refuse me, *pequeña*?' he asked softly.

It took Dorcas a moment or two to find the words to answer him, then she shook her head slowly. 'I—I don't think so—thank you, *señor*,' she said a little hazily.

'*Bien!*' The brief expression of satisfaction was accompanied by a smile as he looked down at the perfume spilled on the pavement at their feet. 'First,' he decided, 'you will allow me to replace your perfume, *verdad*?'

'But I couldn't let——' she began, only to be silenced by a raised hand.

'This time I am sure that I was to blame,' he told her quietly, and with a glint in his eyes that promised laughter. 'You were so very anxious to avoid me, *amante*, and I would like to know why. Perhaps you will tell me while we drive home.'

Dorcas said nothing, but simply walked with

him through the crowded sunny square. His hand was under her arm, and it felt so right somehow to be walking with him like that, so much so that she found herself wishing the walk to the *perfumeria* was longer than it was. Julio Valdares, she decided a little hazily, was not only forceful but irresistible too, and she really ought to be able to do something about her present amenability.

The drive from San Julio had never before seemed so short, and it seemed no more than minutes after they left the little town that the private road to Casa de las Rosas came into view. All the way from town, Dorcas had watched him from the corner of her eye, excitingly aware of that aura of forceful masculinity about him, and the warmth and vigour of that powerful body as he drove the big car along the narrow dusty roads.

She had enjoyed driving with Rafael, but somehow the same journey with Julio had a new dimension and her senses responded to him in a way that not only excited but alarmed her. The strong brown hands that emerged from the cuffs of a pale fawn jacket had a sensual look somehow, and with every movement of his arms the powerful muscles rippled under the light jacket, suggesting an almost contemptuous air of confidence.

There was something powerful, irresistible and essentially masculine about Julio Valdares that she was bound to be affected by, no matter how she tried to resist. Something she found increasingly hard to ignore, the more she came into contact with him.

He turned the car along the narrow road, bord-

ered with palms and lemon trees, and curving upwards towards the villa, hidden behind its *patio*
walls. In front of the high wrought iron gates he
brought the car to a standstill, but instead of getting out, he turned in his seat to look at her.

For several seconds he said nothing, and Dorcas
bore the scrutiny of those dark eyes as best she
could, her hands curled tightly into her palms and
a flush of bright pink on her cheeks that betrayed
the wildly beating heart against her ribs. Then he
half smiled, and she took a short, involuntary
breath as she prepared for questions, for she felt
sure he was going to ask about that allusion Rafael
had made to the *fiesta*; he was bound to be both
interested and curious.

One elbow rested on the steering wheel and he
pinched his lower lip between finger and thumb as
he studied her, his eyes speculative. 'You will not
do anything—foolish, *amante*, will you?' he asked
softly, and Dorcas looked at him with wide eyes for
a moment before lowering her gaze.

'I—I don't know what you're talking about,' she
said, and he shook his head.

'Rafael Montez spoke to you of the *fiesta*,' he said
quietly. 'He—warned you, did he not, Dorcas?'

'In a way.'

He nodded, as if the admission was what he expected. Then with one finger he reached out and
stroked her cheek gently, an evocative, disturbing
touch that sent little shivers of response through
her whole body. 'And why should he warn you, *mi
pequeña*?' he asked softly. 'For what reason would
he warn you about the *fiesta*, hmm?'

Dorcas's thoughts were in chaos as she sat there

feeling incredibly small and helpless beside him. They sat in the shade of the palms beside the gates, close together on the long seat, and she was more nervous than she had ever been in her life as she faced the prospect of telling him what she had recklessly told Rafael.

It was hard to believe that he was the same man she had so formally exchanged greetings with each morning for several months. During the past few days things had moved with such alarming speed that she seemed to have lived a lifetime in them, and she had the strangest feeling that she knew him much better than she did Rafael with whom she had been in much closer contact.

That lighter mark on his neck where the skin had been burned, and the similar scar on the back of his right hand, they were familiar to her, as were the strong, arrogant features and the dark eyes that were still watching her with a kind of gentle speculation, as if she puzzled him.

'*Amante?*' His use of such endearments, too, was another thing she really ought to object to but somehow did not have the heart. *Amante*—a word for lovers yet one which he had used twice within the past few minutes.

'Julio——'

One big hand cupped her chin and turned her to face him, cutting short her half-hearted objection to being questioned, and the hand that turned her face brought their bodies into closer proximity so that her pulses raced wildly as she tried not to look at him. 'You have not promised to ride with Rafael Montez?' he asked quietly, and despite the softness of his voice she detected a hint of steel there too, and his fingers on her jaw tightened their hold briefly too.

'No, of course I haven't promised him!' Dorcas denied. 'I told you that!'

He leaned forward slightly, so that his breath warmed her mouth as he spoke. 'Then why,' he asked, 'are you so nervous, *pequeña*? If it is not a conscience about Rafael that makes you so uneasy, then what is it, hmm?'

Dorcas moved her head, determinedly evading that persuasive hand on her chin, and looked down at the packages on her lap. Her breathing was short and uneven and she felt far more excited than nervous, as he accused her of being. 'You—you have no right to question me like this,' she told him in a small breathless voice. 'No right at all!'

'You are wrong,' Julio argued with a small crooked smile as he shook his head. 'I have the same right that lets me deny Rafael Montez the pleasure of riding with you in the parade, *mi poco tizón*! He is betrothed to my niece, Elena, and until he is man enough to break the contract in an honest way, then he is not free to take you or any other young woman anywhere that you are likely to be seen together, and the wrong construction put upon your relationship. I love Elena and I will not allow her to be hurt, *mi pequeña*, even by you!'

That 'even by you' had a strangely intimate sound that set Dorcas's heart beating even more rapidly and she flicked him an anxious glance as she sought to assure him. 'I—I wouldn't do anything to hurt Elena,' she insisted. 'I liked her and I wouldn't dream of doing anything to deliberately

147

hurt her!'

'*No, claro que no*,' he said softly, and touched her cheek lightly with his fingertips. 'Then I must ask myself who is to be your companion at the *fiesta, mi pequeña*. And do not deny me that right also, Dorcas,' he added when she would have done just that. 'Your brother will understand that concern is necessary now that I have overheard you warned about riding in the parade with some man who is unknown.'

'Oh, he's not un*known*!' Dorcas informed him swiftly and without stopping to think of the consequences. 'Certainly not by you, Don Julio!'

For a moment he said nothing, so that she guessed her answer had puzzled him and it was only now that she realised she had no option now but to tell him that she had claimed him as her partner in the parade, and her whole being trembled at the prospect. A large hand reached over and was laid gently over her own two where they lay in her lap, bringing a swift and urgent reaction from her heart.

'Dorcas,' he said, 'must I ask Rafael Montez who this man is—or shall *I* tell *you, amante*?' He leaned further forward in his seat and squeezed her hands. 'Am I conceited to think that this concerns me, *pequeña*?'

'Don Julio——'

'Answer me, *por favor, amante*,' the quiet voice insisted, and Dorcas looked down at the strong brown fingers curled persuasively over her own.

She could feel her heart hammering with relentless force against her ribs and the pulse at her temple pounded so loudly that her head throbbed with it. There was no way out now and she took a deep breath before responding to the gentle, insistent pressure of his hand.

'It—it does concern you,' she said after a moment or two, and he expressed a deep sigh of satisfaction, although whether because he was right or for some other reason, Dorcas did not know. She took another second to find the right words to explain, then told him the truth. 'I—I did it because Rafael was insisting that I ride with him in the parade,' she said in a small breathless voice. 'I told him I wouldn't—I *couldn't* because——' She looked up at him at last and searched the dark face for some clue to his reaction. 'I told him I was riding with you,' she concluded in a breathless whisper.

'Dorcas——'

'I didn't mean it, of course,' she went on rapidly, without giving him time to say anything. 'It was simply an excuse, Don Julio, and I hope you'll understand why I did it.' She looked up at him again and her eyes pleaded for his understanding. 'I *had* to tell him something quickly before he talked me into going with him,' she confessed, 'and —and so I told him I was going with you as the first thing that came into my head.'

For a moment he said nothing and she wondered if he was very angry. There was nothing that suggested anger in the look on his face, although lowered lids hid the expression in his eyes, and after a moment he took one of her hands and held it lightly in his, the fingers spread as he twined his own strong ones between them, holding them to the warmth of his chest where she could feel his heart beat.

'And are you riding with me, *amante*?' he asked her.

Dorcas looked up swiftly, then hastily looked away again. It was useless to try and guess what he wanted her to say, but something in that deep, quiet voice gave her a strange feeling of elation that trembled through her whole being. 'No, no, of course I can't,' she said breathlessly. 'You always ride alone, Don Julio, you told me so. I—I didn't mean to embarrass you, but I had to tell Rafael something and I just——'

'Used me as an excuse,' Julio interrupted softly, and the fingers holding hers crushed them to his breast. 'I do not permit anyone to make use of me, *poco pichón*,' he went on quietly. 'If you have said you will ride with me, then you will!'

Dorcas's heart was hammering wildly and her mouth was parted as she gazed at him in blank disbelief. 'But—but it wasn't meant to be serious,' she objected breathlessly. 'I wasn't trying to—oh no, you can't take it seriously!'

For a moment the dark eyes looked down at her as if he sought to discover just how serious her objections were, then he shook his head and there was a hint of steel in the hand that held hers so firmly. 'Have you some personal objection to riding with me, *pequeña*?' he asked, and Dorcas shook her head vaguely, her heart beating furiously hard in her breast.

'But——' She sought for words wildly, anxious for him to realise what he was doing, although it was barely credible that he did not already know, in view of the warnings he had issued to Rafael. 'Don Julio, if I did come with you—if I rode with you in the parade, people would think——'

'That I have chosen the most beautiful girl in San Julio for my partner,' he interrupted her. 'And who could deny my right to you, *amante*? It is my saint's day, my choice who rides with me, and I cannot imagine even Rafael Montez having sufficient nerve to challenge me in the circumstances!'

'But——'

'You least of all will deny me, *mi poco pichón*,' Julio insisted quietly, and moved even nearer until his body pressed her hard against the leather upholstery, his arms drawing her into a circle that could not be broken, steely hard and irresistible.

His mouth sought hers, fierce and hard, parting her lips and smothering the small vague cry she made as she closed her eyes, enveloped in that spicy male tanginess that did strange and inexplicable things to her emotions. He kissed her fiercely and passionately, and she felt herself yield to the hard pressure of his body as she slid her arms up round his neck, wanting this more than anything in the world at the moment and very unwillingly letting him go when he gently eased her to arm's length suddenly.

The dark eyes looked at her for a second, glittering and unfathomable, then he smiled slowly, his eyes crinkling at their corners in that fascinating and intriguing way they always did. 'I will tell your brother that you will ride with me, *pequeña*,' he said. 'He will understand.'

Dorcas, bewildered and not quite knowing what she felt, looked at him for a moment, wishing she understood as well as he seemed confident Ramón would. 'I——' she began, but he was shaking his head, and she yielded to the warmth of his body again briefly when he leaned across and opened the car door for her.

'*Hasta mañana, amante,*' he breathed softly in her ear, and Dorcas got out of the car in a daze. She was no longer very sure of anything, least of all her feelings for Don Julio Valdares.

CHAPTER EIGHT

It was impossible to avoid noticing that Ramón was watching her across the table in a curiously speculative way, and Dorcas wondered what was on his mind. It was obvious that something was and no doubt sooner or later he would enlighten her; in the meantime she was enjoying her dinner.

The table, sumptuous with snowy linen and the beautiful old silver left to Ramón by his grandmother, was lit by overhead lamps of beaten brass, and they lent a soft glow to the whole room, echoing the mood of the evening.

Through the open windows the scents and sounds of the *patio* heightened the air of peace and wellbeing, and yet Dorcas wondered why she felt so strangely restless. The perfume of roses and magnolias was almost as heady as the wine that Ramón poured from the glass *jarrita*, and the *grillos* chirped a background to the light breath of wind that stirred the trees into lazy response. It was a perfect, beautiful night, and yet she found it impossible to relax.

Ramón's dark eyes studied her for a moment longer while he ate a mouthful of *menestra de pollo*, and Dorcas suffered the scrutiny while she too appreciated the cook's skill with chicken and vegetables. 'Why did you not tell me, *niña*, that you had consented to partner Don Julio Valdares in *la cabalgada*?' Ramón asked her at last, and immediately aroused Doña Teresa's interest.

'Is this true, *mi niña*?' she asked, and it was evident that the idea pleased her. She had always been a staunch admirer of Julio's, of course, and the fact that Dorcas was at last showing sufficient good sense to be friendly towards him would please her even more than it did Ramón. There was no doubt Ramón was pleased, it was obvious from his manner in broaching the subject, and that alone made Dorcas curious to some extent.

She had expected surprise, perhaps even disapproval, if the tradition of the parade was all that Rafael and Julio said it was, and that was why she had delayed telling them about it, for fear of their reactions. Instead neither of them seemed in the least surprised or put out that she was probably going to compromise herself irrevocably by sharing Don Julio's mount with all San Julio looking on.

It was only now that the full meaning of what she had to face came home to her, and she felt a strange curling sensation in her stomach at the prospect of being perched up there behind Julio Valdares, an arm around his waist, while he showed off both her and his horsemanship to the watching crowds.

Doña Teresa's neat grey head was tilted to one side as she regarded first her nephew and then Dorcas with bright dark eyes, and her soft voice brought Dorcas out of her daydream. 'Dorcas?' she prompted gently, and Dorcas took a moment more to consider.

She would rather have told Ramón in her own

good time about taking part in the parade, but it was typical of Julio, of course, to have forestalled her. She had no doubt at all that he was Ramón's informant, and it was probably his way of making sure that she did not have second thoughts before the event. 'I suppose Julio told you?' she guessed, and Ramón nodded.

'When I saw him this morning,' he agreed quietly.

Surprised, she blinked at him. 'This morning?' she echoed. She had gone into San Julio briefly this morning, on an errand for Ramón, but somehow the idea of Julio having called while she was out was not only disappointing but puzzling as well. 'You didn't say he'd been here again,' she said, and Ramón looked at her with a lurking gleam of amusement in his eyes.

'Did I not?' he asked blandly. 'You were out, niña, or you would have seen him.'

A small cold niggle of suspicion gnawed at Dorcas's mind and she looked at her brother searchingly. 'It's odd he should call again so soon,' she told him. 'Or did he come especially to tell you about—about me?'

Ramón smiled. 'He called on a matter of business,' he informed her coolly, and Dorcas shook her head. His attitude towards Julio puzzled her lately. In the beginning, she felt sure, his refusal to sell his land had been at least in part because he disliked the man who wanted it so badly, but now she was no longer sure. Recently his whole manner had changed and he had even tried to persuade her to accept Julio as an escort instead of Rafael. Now, she learned, Julio had called yet again at Casa de las Rosas, and on a matter of business, so Ramón said. Something that made her more uneasy than ever.

'You're getting very friendly with him,' she said, and somehow managed to make it sound like an accusation, so that once again Ramón smiled in that knowing, and slightly irritating way.

'I have no quarrel with my neighbour, Dorcas,' he told her gently. 'I have never disliked the man —any animosity was all on your part, *mi poca hermana!*'

Momentarily outfaced, Dorcas gave her attention to her dinner for a second or two, although she had little appetite left. There was something about Ramón's attitude that she found not only disturbing but suspicious, and she could not quell that small niggle of doubt that still gave her butterflies in her stomach. 'I disliked him because he was trying to rob you of your property,' she reminded him defensively, and Ramón shook his head.

'There was never any question of my being robbed, *niña*,' he argued quietly. 'Don Julio wanted to purchase my land and, at that time, I had no wish to sell, that is all.'

His choice of phrase was significant, she recognised and looked at him for a moment, frowning curiously. 'At that time?' she echoed, and glanced at Doña Teresa seeking support, but her eyes were downcast as if she had no further interest in the conversation, something that Dorcas doubted very much. 'Ramón,' she said, 'is there something you haven't told *me*?'

She thought she knew what he was going to tell her, even before he spoke, but she was so unwilling

156

to believe it that she prayed she was wrong. 'I have to face the fact that Casa de las Rosas is no longer a practical proposition as far as I am concerned, Dorcas,' Ramón told her. 'I cannot work the land, and that is a crime in itself, to leave good land lying idle. I cannot in all conscience allow it to go on any longer.'

'You've sold out to him!'

Dorcas could not really have said why it hurt so much, but she suddenly felt like crying. If Julio had pressured her brother into parting with his property at long last it would be an almost unbearable fact to face, for it would be so much harder for her to hate him now, no matter what he did.

In fact Ramón seemed remarkably matter-of-fact, and it occurred to her that he was possibly less attached to the Casa de las Rosas than she was herself. 'I have agreed to sell the Casa de las Rosas, Dorcas,' he said quietly and with a hint of censure in his voice, 'but the decision was entirely mine, not Don Julio's.'

'He—he didn't force you into selling?' She was almost begging him to deny it, she realised, and Ramón smiled.

'It will be much more convenient for me to live nearer to Cádiz and my work,' he pointed out. 'This has been in my mind for some time, Dorcas, but it is a decision I had to make for myself, and there is no question of my having—sold out to anyone. The phrase is much too dramatic to cover a perfectly straightforward business transaction, niña!'

'I'm glad!'

The relief she felt was inestimable and she wondered if Ramón had any idea, for he was smiling at her and shaking his head. 'You do Don Julio an injustice, *pequeña*,' he told her softly, 'if you see him as the kind of man to hound a man to desperation to gain possession of his land, and you also do your brother less than justice. My body may be useless, *poca hermana*, but I am no more easily moved from my own set course than—than Don Julio Valdares!'

'I know!' she assured him. 'But it's just that I can't see you in a small town house. You seem to belong to the Casa de las Rosas somehow!'

Ramón looked around him at the familiar room and smiled. 'One can become accustomed to change, *pequeña*,' he told her softly. 'You will of course come with us and so complete our family, there will be plenty of room.'

Once again Dorcas felt close to tears, and she reached out and covered the hand nearest to her on the table. 'Thank you,' she said. 'I shall miss the Casa de las Rosas, but I should miss you and Tía Teresa more.' She too looked around the big, softly lit room and sighed. 'So Julio has his way after all,' she said.

Ramón's dark eyes were speculative and he smiled teasingly, squeezing her fingers. 'But you surely prefer that Don Julio has the Casa de las Rosas rather than a stranger, Dorcas?' he suggested. 'If you have consented to ride with him in *la cabalgada*, you cannot claim to dislike him still, hmm?'

Both he and Doña Teresa were watching her with interest, Dorcas realised, Doña Teresa with a gentle, curious look in her eyes, and Ramón as if he knew of something that pleased him, and Dorcas felt her heart suddenly hammering relentlessly hard. She had not until now realised how significant Don Julio's gesture was in allowing her to ride with him, but both Ramón and Doña Teresa seemed in no doubt, and she carefully avoided looking at either of them as she went back to her neglected meal.

'There's nothing significant in my riding with Julio,' she said, carefully prodding up a last morsel of chicken. 'He didn't ask me, you know, it was a—a fluke really.'

Doña Teresa looked at her nephew for a translation, but he too was puzzled, and he shrugged vaguely. 'I do not understand, Dorcas.'

'I—I just used him as an excuse,' she explained. 'I expected him to be furious about it, but he wasn't.'

She had never really given it much thought until now, but simply been grateful that he hadn't been as angry as she expected. He had inveigled the information from her, but instead of losing his temper at her temerity in using him, he had insisted that she make her rash claim to Rafael a fact.

'*Madre mi!*' Ramón swore softly. 'If you mean what I think you mean, Dorcas——'

'I do!' she insisted a little defiantly, so that Ramón frowned.

'Then he had every right to be angry if you made such a claim without foundation!' he told her, and Dorcas nodded.

'I know he had,' she agreed reluctantly, 'but Rafael was pressing me hard to ride with him, and I didn't know what to do! I thought about Elena and how she'd feel, and I couldn't agree, but

Rafael didn't seem to care, and he——' She shrugged, not wanting to make Rafael appear too callous, although she wondered if it wasn't an accurate description in view of his readiness to abandon Elena in her favour. 'It was difficult to make him understand that I meant what I said,' she insisted, 'so I told him I was riding with Julio.'

Doña Teresa seemed to have abandoned her meal altogether, and she stared at Dorcas with dark, incredulous eyes. 'You involved Don Julio without his knowing anything about it?' she asked, and shook her head reproachfully. 'That was wrong, *niña*, it was very wrong of you!'

'I know, I know!' Dorcas's lip trembled when she thought of her moment of panic, how she had fled when she saw Julio paying off her taxi-driver. 'I—I just wanted Rafael to stop bothering me, that's all, Tía Teresa!'

'But did you not realise,' Doña Teresa pointed out gently, 'that being the man he is, he would have no other choice but to support your claim?'

'Oh!' The idea stunned her for a moment, and Dorcas looked at Ramón, her eyes wide and appealing, unwilling to believe that mere good manners had made Julio agree to take her with him in the parade. 'Oh, Ramón, no!'

His fingers curled strongly and comfortingly over hers and he smiled. 'No, *niña*,' he assured her softly but confidently. 'I think I know Don Julio well enough to assure you that he would not have agreed to the idea if it was not to his liking.' Dorcas, only too willing to be convinced, sighed her relief and even managed a smile. 'But you had no right to involve him as you did,' Ramón went on, determined to impress her with the fact, and again she nodded agreement.

'I didn't even mean him to know about it,' she confessed. 'But he came along while I was with Rafael, and Rafael almost gave me away!'

Ramón squeezed her fingers gently. 'And Don Julio Valdares is very—persuasive, is he not, *pequeña?*' he whispered, and Dorcas was bound to agree.

'He was horrible to Rafael because he hurt my wrist,' she said, and absently rubbed the wrist where Rafael had held her so hurtfully tight. She coped with a sudden and unexpected tingle of excitement when she remembered how angry Julio had been about that. 'And he paid off my taxi, which was what Rafael had meant to do, then drove me home himself.'

'It seems to me,' Ramón decided in a quiet voice, 'that Señor Montez takes a great many liberties!'

Dorcas felt suddenly as if a weight had been lifted from her shoulders, although for no good reason that she could think of, and as she lifted her fork to her lips her eyes met Ramón's briefly, almost challengingly. 'No more than Julio Valdares does,' she argued, and Ramón frowned.

'There is a difference,' he reminded her in a firm reproachful voice. 'Rafael Montez is betrothed to another woman, Don Julio is not!'

Carefully placing her knife and fork neatly together on her empty plate, Dorcas dabbed her mouth, then took up her wine glass and held it in both hands while she brushed its cool edge against her lips. 'I wonder why not,' she said, as much to herself as to Ramón, and he frowned curiously.

'*No entiendo*,' he said.

Dorcas smiled slowly as she brushed the cool glass against her mouth. 'He's very attractive,' she told him. 'I sometimes wonder why he's still single —or was there ever a Señora Valdares?'

'Not to my knowledge,' Ramón told her, and she knew from that little frown and the edge of anxiety on his voice that he was worried about her curiosity. 'Dorcas,' he said, 'you will not—you will not ask him about such a thing?'

'Oh, of course not!' She sipped her wine, then gazed down into the empty glass for a moment, more curious about a possible Señora Valdares than she cared to admit. 'I just wondered,' she said, and was surprised to find just how much it mattered to her whether or not Julio Valdares had ever been married.

It took Dorcas quite a time to decide to follow her usual practice of walking in the old olive grove the next morning and she was completely at loss when she eventually left the house, to know whether she hoped to see Julio Valdares or not.

The bright copper-blue sky was so bright that she narrowed her eyes when she tried to look up at it, so she directed her gaze instead to a less dazzling point of interest. Just below where she was walking the grove swept inwards, enfolding part of Julio's estate, and the dusty green of the eucalyptus trees was much more restful to her eyes.

It was just about in that spot that Julio would appear if he was going to put in an appearance this morning, and if he was riding at his customary time, he would be along at any minute. Realising that she was actually watching for him, she pulled herself up sharply and feigned an interest in other aspects of the landscape.

In contrast to the pale, arid soil in the old grove, the land on Julio's side was pasture, not lush by English standards, but good in a countryside where every scrap of growth was dependent upon irrigation. Then suddenly, as her eyes strayed across the far side again, he came into view as if from nowhere, and she was faced with the choice of going on and making their usual meeting inevitable, or turning back now, before he got close enough to see her.

She shaded her eyes for a moment with one hand, and gazed at the approaching figure, her heart pounding urgently in her breast, then she lowered her hand again and sighed. She simply hadn't the strength of will or the inclination to deliberately avoid him, and recognising the fact seemed as inevitable as their meeting.

It was only a minute later when he once more came into sight on the other side of the narrow border of trees, and Dorcas almost held her breath until he turned his head and looked at her. He did not dismount, as she half expected he would, but came towards her through the trees still mounted on the beautiful golden-cream stallion he rode. He said nothing for a moment, but reined in beside her, his dark eyes seeking and holding hers for a brief, heart-stopping minute.

Fawn trousers of some thin smooth material and long brown boots revealed the muscular strength of his long legs, and the shirt he wore fitted closely across his broad chest and back. It was almost inevitable that her eyes strayed to those faint ugly scars that marred the smooth dusky gold of his skin below his jaw and on the back of his right hand, and she hastily looked away again because the sight of them disturbed her strangely.

The strong dark hands on the reins looked deceptively at ease, but the stallion he rode was in no doubt who was in control. He tried to toss his silky mane in spite of the hard Spanish bit, but achieved little and shifted impatiently while Julio looked down, trying in vain to hold Dorcas's gaze as easily as he did his mount.

'*Buenos dias*, Dorcas,' he said, and that deep, quiet voice played havoc with her senses, as it always did.

'*Buenos dias*.'

She stopped short of using his christian name, although she had done so easily enough when she talked about him to Doña Teresa and Ramon, and she realised how obvious the omission was when he laughed. The sound of his laughter was new to her and it both surprised and disturbed her so that she looked up swiftly.

A myriad small lines radiated from the corners of his eyes and his teeth showed startlingly white in that dusky, hawkish face so that she was again reminded of that pirate image she had endowed him with what seemed like a lifetime ago. 'Do you find it so difficult to pronounce my name, *niña*?' he asked, and Dorcas hastily shook her head to deny it.

'No, of course not, *señor*!'

'*Señor*?' He raised a black brow and shook his

head, his eyes still glittering with laughter. 'So formal, *niña*, when you are to be my——' Another raised brow and an expressive shrug of his shoulders left the choice to her, and Dorcas wished she knew exactly what she had let herself in for when she made that rash statement to Rafael.

She controlled her voice with some difficulty, inwardly sympathising with the stallion's desire to be away from there. There was something about Julio Valdares this morning, some indefinable aura of magnetism that stirred her senses into chaos, and yet she could not yet put her finger on what it was that set her heart pounding and made her legs tremble as if at any moment they would let her down. Nor was it easy to appear confident and assured when she was so far below him that she had to tip back her head to look at him.

'My aunt suggested that you had little choice but to—to agree to my riding with you,' she said in as firm a voice as she could manage. 'She thinks that I forced your hand by telling Rafael what I did and that you're simply being polite in following the idea through.'

He said nothing for a moment and she chanced a brief upward glance through her lashes at the shadowy darkness of his face. He seemed not a bit put out by the suggestion, though perhaps a little more thoughtful, but it was difficult to tell in such a brief glance. 'Doña Teresa scolded you?' he asked quietly, and she shook her head.

'Not exactly, but——' Again she looked up at him. 'Both she and Ramón said you had every right to be as angry as I expected you to be.'

'So!' He leaned forward slightly, resting one arm

across the saddle, and the long Spanish quirt he carried slid beneath her chin, raising her face to him. 'You expected me to be angry with you, eh, *niña*? And did you, too, think I had the right to be angry?'

The plaited leather was cool on her skin and Dorcas put up a hand to move it aside, glancing up at him as she did so. 'I suppose so,' she admitted frankly, and again his sudden laugh startled her.

'You suppose so, *impudencia*? Why then do you suppose I am not, huh?'

Dorcas shook her head. The stallion had shifted uneasily at the sound of that deep, soft laugh and strong hands pulled him round again relentlessly. Stepping back, she eyed the animal warily, suddenly wondering if this could be the horse she would be sharing with Julio tomorrow.

'I—I don't know,' she said in answer to his question, and again met his eyes for a brief moment. 'I wanted to tell you,' she said, 'that if you change your mind about it—I mean, I don't want you to feel bound to do something that was none of your doing in the first place. I don't expect you to go on with it just because you're too polite to refuse.'

'I am not, *niña*!' The dark face broke into a smile and her heart leaped wildly in response to it. 'If I did not wish to ride with you I would have told you so, have no doubt of that!' It was true, of course, he would never have let her get away with her claim to be his partner if it had not suited him to do so. Again the leather quirt slid beneath her chin and raised her face to him. 'And please do not think that you may have second thoughts about joining me, *amante*,' he warned softly, 'for be sure

166

I shall come for you!'

She said nothing for a moment, but her mind was trying to cope with a hundred and one doubts now that there was so little time left, and she wondered if she would ever have the nerve to sit up there behind him while they rode through the narrow, crowded streets of San Julio. 'I—I don't know if I can do it,' she told him in a small husky voice, and he frowned.

'*Por qué no?*' he demanded, and even Dorcas's Spanish could make sense of that.

She stood below him, her hands tightly together and her fair head bent so that she need not look at him while she made her excuses. 'I—I'm scared,' she admitted frankly, and yet again looked up swiftly when he laughed.

'Of me, *amante?*' he asked softly. 'Or of the horse?'

Stung into being on the defensive, she lifted her chin and looked at him steadily. 'Perhaps of both, *señor!*' she retorted, and turned away. Her hands and legs were trembling like leaves and there was a rapid urgent beat in her heart as she walked across to stand in the deeper shade of a low-growing young plane tree, with her back to him.

She heard an indignant snort of impatience from the stallion and the next moment Julio was behind her, on foot, twisting her swiftly round to face him. His hands held her firmly around her slim waist and pulled her against the steely warmth of his body, then he looked at her for a moment with those glittering dark eyes before he bent his head, and his mouth when it touched hers was unexpectedly gentle.

She made no effort to push him away or to struggle, and one big hand cradled the back of her head while his other arm circled her slender waist, drawing her close until she could feel the warmth of his body through the thin shirt and the steady beat of his heart under her hands. He kissed her gently and yet with a hint of such fierce passion that her head spun with its promise.

Then slowly he released her and his hands cupped her face while he looked down into her eyes as she slowly opened them again. 'You have no need to fear either of us, *mi pichón*,' he said softly. 'You will be safe with me—will you not trust me?' Silently Dorcas nodded, and he bent his head again briefly and kissed her forehead. '*Hasta mañana, mi amar*,' he whispered.

She thought he would have said more, but he shook his head after a moment's hesitation and walked away from her back to where his horse stood waiting. Turning just before he mounted, he smiled at her and raised a hand, and Dorcas watched him swing easily into the saddle.

'*Hasta mañana*,' she said softly as he rode off.

CHAPTER NINE

DORCAS had looked at her reflection a hundred times in the mirror before she left her bedroom, and found it hard to believe that the girl who looked out at her was the same one who had come from England only a little over three months ago. Her skin had tanned to a pale gold that went well with her fair hair and blue eyes, and the flounced, wide-sleeved dress she wore was like nothing she had ever owned before.

The dress had been Doña Teresa's present to her, a special dress for her to wear in the parade, and at first she had to get used to the completely different image it gave her. Not that it made her appear at all Spanish, with her colouring that wasn't possible, but it did give her a distinctly different feeling that was part of the general sense of excitement she felt.

The dress was made in red and white silk with the simply cut bodice of the traditional Spanish costume. It clung to the soft curves of her body as far as her hips then flared out into multiple layers of deep frills edged with red, which whirled out from her slim legs when she spun round. It had a couple of deep flounces round the short sleeves too, and a scooped-out neckline. She felt strange and rather exotic in it and yet at the same time curiously at ease, once she got used to it.

She wore her long fair hair loose about her shoulders and very little make-up so that she looked rather less than her twenty-one years. When Julio first saw her he murmured something in Spanish about her being a beautiful child, but it was obvious from the dark gleam in his eyes that he appreciated the way she looked, and that was enough to set her pulses racing.

San Julio in *fiesta* costume was quite different from the quiet and somewhat sleepy little town she was more familiar with, and she felt a tingling excitement as they moved off to join the other riders in the *cabalgada*. Every one of the tall, narrow houses through the little town's congested streets was draped with colourful flags and streamers, and their iron balconies were crowded with watchers, suspended above the heads of those milling closely together in good-natured chaos on the pavements below.

Ahead of them the procession wound its way, a long cavalcade of tableaux and walkers, riders and tumblers. Giant-headed monsters pranced and charged at any pretty girl who caught their eye, their grotesque heads bobbing almost as high as the lower balconies, and open carriages were filled with pretty girls wearing the traditional Andalusian costume of red and white flounced dresses, such as Dorcas wore, waving and smiling as they acknowledged the cheering approval of the crowds.

Dorcas felt quite sickeningly nervous when she first climbed up behind Julio on the back of a beautiful dark brown mare who was only slightly less head-tossingly wilful than the stallions he more normally rode. The mare too was dressed for the occasion with a long leather fringe decorating her headstall and her saddle decorated and embossed with gilt studs and scrollwork, her coat shining like brown satin from good grooming.

All around them were other riders, some with their *novias* riding behind them and some riding alone, as Julio would most likely have been had Dorcas not made that rash, impulsive claim to Rafael. She thought of Rafael only briefly, and then only when she thought she caught a glimpse of him among the other riders just before they moved off.

The room for two to ride on the mare's back was limited and at first Dorcas had been hesitant about sitting too close to Julio. One or two near slips, however, had made her realise that it simply wasn't possible to keep at a distance in the circumstances and she now sat as close as she could get with one arm curved about his lean waist as she saw the other girls doing, her slim brown legs below the frilled skirt swinging down over the mare's left flank.

It was evident from the looks she had drawn so far that her obviously Anglo-Saxon colouring was going to cause a deal of comment, and that too had initially made her shy of going through with it. It came to her again too, in the moment that they moved off to join the cavalcade, that by riding behind him in the traditional manner she was putting both herself and Julio in a curiously delicate position, and for a few moments she almost panicked. Only now it was too late to go back and soon all San Julio and hundreds of visitors too would see them making a public declaration of something that did not even exist.

There was no mistaking Julio for anything other than the typical Spanish don, and it surprised Dorcas in the first few moments of realisation that she was as proud to be seen with him as any of the Spanish girls were who rode with their *novios*. The severe but attractive traditional Andalusian riding costume suited him perfectly, and his air of arrogant self-confidence was a perfect complement to it.

Black, tight-fitting trousers with a cummerbund swathed about his lean waist and short black boots made him appear even taller than usual, and were worn with a short, fitted black jacket. It was basically a rather severe costume, but it was lent a touch of romanticism by a white shirt that was ruffled at the neck and wrists and did a lot to soften the air of severity.

She had never before seen him wear a hat, but the wide, stiff-brimmed Córdoban hat set at a jaunty angle over his brow gave him a rakish air that ideally suited his dark, strong features and somehow served to increase her own trembling air of excitement.

As they turned into the Plaza de San Julio he turned his head and looked over his shoulder at her, and she wondered if he too was remembering their first significant encounter in the little church now half hidden by a milling crowd of watchers. One brow was raised in query and she responded with a smile, her eyes bright and glowing, with a soft pink glow in her cheeks.

'*Usted es hermosa!*' he said softly, and Dorcas took the tone of his voice as an indication of the words. Something, he was telling her, was beautiful, and from that warm, dark gleam in his eyes it was obvious enough that the compliment was meant for her.

'I'm enjoying myself,' she confessed, and for no other reason than that she felt deliriously and lightheartedly happy suddenly, she laughed and hugged up closer still to the broad back.

'*Bien!*' His dark eyes glittered like jet in the shadow of the Córdoban hat and the white gleam of his teeth in that dusky face betrayed a smile. 'Did I not tell you that there was nothing to fear?' he asked, and Dorcas nodded without speaking. Sitting so close to him she was pressed close against the warm strength of his body, her fingertips picking up the beat of his heart through the frilled shirt. Whatever feelings she might have had about Julio Valdares in the past months, there was absolutely no doubt in her mind as she rode with him through the bright, noisy streets of San Julio that she had never in her life felt about anyone the way she did about him at the moment.

Her heart raced wildly in time with the high-stepping, excited progress of the brown mare, and her brain spun in a chaotic jumble of emotions and realisations. Some hint of the way she was feeling must have communicated itself in some way to Julio too, for he turned again suddenly and for a long moment held her gaze without smiling, his eyes moving at last to search every inch of her flushed face and lingering longest on her mouth.

'Dorcas, *mi amar!*' he breathed softly, and she suddenly bent her head and buried her face against his broad back, her encircling arm curved more tightly while her fingers moved slowly and sooth-ingly over the place where his dark flesh was burned into a jagged scar.

She said nothing, but her heart was so incredibly light and it beat so hard in her breast that she felt sure he must feel it as she hugged her body as close to him as she could. The crowds, the banners and the millions of flowers that lay scattered before them on the narrow, sunny streets were suddenly significant of so much more than a public *fiesta*. They were part of Julio's world and he was sud-denly and inescapably the most important part of hers.

He rode as he always rode, with his head held high and proudly arrogant, and his strong brown hands controlling the well-bred skittishness of his mount with an ease that amounted almost to con-tempt, but never before had Dorcas felt so com-pletely in tune with him.

A watcher on one of the crowded balconies above them threw down a rose as a compliment to her fairness among his countrymen's Latin darkness, and Dorcas caught it with a smile and waved her thanks. To the delight of the donor she tucked the flower behind her ear with a bravado that she would never have thought herself capable of, even yesterday.

The music, the noise and the excitement whirled around her in a kaleidoscope of colour and sound and she had never felt so incredibly happy in her life before. Then suddenly, as if appearing from nowhere, Rafael was beside them, mounted on a silky black mare and with Elena sitting close be-hind him, her dark eyes glowing softly.

She smiled at Dorcas and at her uncle, as if all was well with her world, and Dorcas thought she knew exactly how she felt. '*Olà!*' Elena spoke above the noise, and her eyes went swiftly and meaningfully between Dorcas and her uncle.

Unable to disguise anything in her present mood, Dorcas smiled and returned the greeting, noticing as she did so that Rafael looked much less disgruntled and resentful than he had of late. In fact he was smiling and his expression when he looked at Dorcas was a strange blend of sheepishness and defiance, although the latter was intended more for Julio, she suspected.

What she had hoped for had, to all appearances, happened. Having resigned himself to appearing with Elena in public as his *novia*, he quite liked the idea and seemed to be enjoying himself. Dorcas, more relieved than she could say, smiled at him encouragingly. '*Mucha suerte*, Rafael,' she told him, as quietly as it was possible to and still be heard above the noise of the crowd, and Rafael too smiled and inclined his head in that brief, formal bow she was so familiar with.

'*Gracias, chica,*' he replied, and waited to hear no more but spurred his horse further ahead of them, with Elena smiling and waving as they disappeared into the throng of riders and carriages.

'You wish him good luck, *amante*?' Julio asked over his shoulder, and Dorcas noticed how easily the endearment came to his lips and how willingly she accepted it.

'Of course,' she told him softly. 'He knows he belongs with Elena, Julio, and I don't think he'll forget it again now.'

Briefly the dark face broke into a smile that crinkled his eyes at their corners, touching his strong features with a gentleness that set her heart skipping. 'I do not think he will ever be so tempted again, *mi amar*,' he said softly, and took one hand from the rein briefly, to press her hand even closer to his breast. '*Dios gracias!*' he added in a whisper, and raised her fingers briefly to his lips.

It was so quiet after the noise and excitement of the *fiesta* and Dorcas leaned back against the seat of the car for a moment and gazed out at the huge boldness of the moon in a velvety sky. The moon and stars were in sole possession again now that the fireworks were finished and the night looked unbelievably tranquil after the wild emotionalism of the past few hours.

She had spent more than seven hours, riding, walking, watching tableaux and hundreds of fireworks, until her head spun with the glamour and excitement of it all, but still she wasn't tired—she had never been less tired in her life. Doña Teresa in the back seat of the car looked as if the hours had taken a heavier toll of her energies, but she too had enjoyed herself, Dorcas was convinced, and she smiled now when Dorcas turned and looked at her.

'I wish Ramón could have been with us,' she said, her eyes bright and glowing. 'He would have loved it!' She looked ahead again at the distant hill where the Casa de las Rosas stood, just below its more opulent neighbour, Julio's Las Furias, and as yet out of sight. 'I wonder if he could see the fireworks from his window.'

'Perhaps, *niña*,' Doña Teresa said quietly, smiling and tolerant of her excitement. 'Luis, his valet, will have helped him into bed before he left to see the fireworks and he is probably resting.'

'He's all alone,' said Dorcas, and her pity for her deserted brother was plain in her voice. 'It's such a shame one of the servants couldn't have stayed with him.'

Doña Teresa shook her head. 'Ramón is always most anxious that they all see at least some of the *fiesta*,' she told her. 'It is the most important day of the year in San Julio and he would not deprive them of their right to be there.'

'I know,' Dorcas said, 'but I felt a bit guilty about leaving him when I knew he'd be alone for several hours tonight.'

'Do not worry, *niña*,' Doña Teresa said softly, and reached over to touch her shoulder gently. 'You will tell him about it when we return, hmm?'

Dorcas settled back in her seat again and sighed. 'I can't quite believe it's all happened,' she said. and laughed as she shook her head. 'I've seen so much and learned so much; I've become——' She stopped short there and laughed a little light-headedly. 'It's been like stepping into another world!'

Doña Teresa smiled, as if she understood her re-action exactly, but it was Julio who answered her, turning his head for a moment to look at her with those dark expressive eyes glowing like coals in the dim light. 'You have enjoyed this—other world, *niña*?' he asked, and Dorcas nodded.

'I've enjoyed every minute!' she declared with-out hesitation, and looked at him from the shadows of her lashes, wondering if she dare attribute her main enjoyment to being with him. She was still not sure enough of him to let him know exactly how she felt, but the temptation was there to tell him.

He smiled, one of those eye-crinkling smiles that set her pulses racing even when it was barely discernible for the lack of illumination. Her heart was hammering wildly and she studied him for a moment as he drove them along the narrow, moonlit road up from San Julio.

In the vague, dim light that was all the windows of the car admitted, his face appeared as little more than a dusky outline against the window the other side of him. Harsh and unrelenting, she would have said, had she not known him better, and marvelled suddenly at how quickly she had got to know him better. It seemed like only yesterday that she had hated him for trying to buy Ramón's land from him, and now today she had admitted, though only to herself so far, that she loved him more than anyone in the world.

He turned his head again suddenly and a glimpse of white teeth betrayed another smile. 'Are you not tired?' he asked, and Dorcas shook her head.

She was all too aware of Doña Teresa sitting behind them, and for the first time since she had known her, wished she was anywhere else but in her company. 'I'm not a bit tired!' she declared. 'I could go on all night—but Tía Teresa couldn't!' She glanced over her shoulder at Doña Teresa and laughed. 'It's tiring work being chaperone to me, isn't it, Tía Teresa?'

'It is tiring but very pleasant,' Doña Teresa admitted with a smile. 'And I too have enjoyed this *fiesta, niña*, more than I have enjoyed one for many years.'

'I'm glad!' Dorcas glanced behind her and smiled. 'It's all been so new to me, and so exciting. I feel it's been a very special day, somehow!'

'A very special day!' Julio echoed softly, and she nodded without words.

There were no words to describe exactly how she felt. How she had felt ever since that moment when he had turned and smiled at her as they passed the little church of San Julio. She had never been in love before; never with such intensity or with such certainty, and she dared not stop and think yet what she would do if Julio's behaviour towards her today had been no more than a response aroused by the general air of festivity.

They turned another bend and the Casa de las Rosas came into sight at last, although in the moonlight it appeared as little more than a darker patch on the hillside with the lighter patch of the arid old olive grove behind it. She smiled when she saw it, then almost at once remembered that it would soon no longer be Ramón's but would belong to Julio, and her feelings were strangely mixed as she watched the distance shrink swiftly until they turned on to the private road to the villa.

'I can see——' She stopped and gasped, unwilling to believe what she saw. 'It's—it's on fire!' she whispered. 'The house is on fire!'

'*Madre de Dios!*' Julio breathed the prayer in a whisper and pressed his foot even harder on to the accelerator while Doña Teresa murmured something in rapid Spanish and hastily crossed herself as she stared ahead to where the betraying red gleam of fire showed at one of the downstairs windows.

'It is Ramón's bedroom!' she whispered, and leaned forward in her seat, her hands clenched urgently. '*Deprisa, señor, deprisa, por favor!*'

The iron gates of the patio barred their going any further than the end of the private road, but as Julio got swiftly out of the car he called back to Dorcas over his shoulder. 'Open the gates, Dorcas, *rapido!* The fire brigade must be called!'

Instinctively Dorcas did as he told her, and the gates stood open by the time he had run across the *patio* to the window where the flames showed vividly bright in the big room beyond. At first the glass was still intact, but she heard it crash outwards at the same moment as she heard the distinctive sound of the fire engines coming along the road from San Julio.

Leaving Doña Teresa by the gates, Dorcas ran after Julio and reached him as he pulled off the short riding jacket he wore and plunged it into the fountain. 'The fire engines are coming!' she told him breathlessly as he wrapped the soaking wet jacket round his head. 'Ramón must have called them from the telephone by his bed!'

'*Bien!*' He turned his head and looked behind him at the licking flames from the now broken window, and for a brief moment Dorcas saw again the same blank look of fear in his eyes that she had noticed that evening when Ramón accidentally dropped a burning match on to a tray rather than burn his fingers.

'Julio!' She clutched at his arm, recognising

with a flick of horror what strength of will it would require from him to enter a burning building again when he still bore the scars of that other conflagration. He wore a look of taut determination that gave his face an unnatural fierceness, but she knew by instinct what agonies of indecision he must be suffering, and the muscles under her fingers were like tensed steel. 'No!' she said urgently. 'No, Julio, you don't have to, the firemen will——'

'I am going to try and get your brother out of there,' Julio told her through tight, bloodless lips. 'There is no time to wait, Dorcas. Now please keep back and let go of my arm!'

He shook his arm free of her restraining hand, almost as if he was angry with her for weakening his resolve, and she could only watch anxiously and helplessly when he plunged in through the door of the villa and disappeared from her sight.

The fire seemed to be retained in the one room so far, and she thanked heaven for that, for Julio's sake if not for Ramón's, but even while she watched, a billow of smoke came rolling out of the door and she choked back a cry, her hands to her mouth. She wanted so much to help, but until the fire engines arrived there was nothing else anyone could do but wait.

More afraid than she had ever been in her life, she was trembling like a leaf as she stood there, unable to take her eyes from the door where Julio had disappeared, and her emotions were in such chaos that she barely even responded to Doña Teresa's gentle touch on her arm. She wanted Ramón safe, of course, but she could not face the possible cost to Julio.

It seemed an interminable time before the fire engines arrived, but when they eventually came they wasted no time. Doña Teresa explained the situation and in a spate of rapid Spanish they set about organising their equipment. It took them a surprisingly short time, Dorcas appreciated, but while they were doing that Julio was in there somewhere, fighting to get Ramón out. A completely helpless man like Ramón was without his chair would be no easy burden to carry and she waited as close as she could get without hindering the fire crew, her hands pressed to her mouth, her eyes fixed, wide and anxious on that empty doorway.

Doña Teresa, sensitive to her anxiety, and perhaps also to her mixed loyalties, put a comforting arm about her shoulders, waiting with her, saying nothing because there was nothing that could be put into words. It was the longest and the hardest few minutes of Dorcas's life, and she felt she aged several years while they lasted. Never before had she experienced anything as traumatic as waiting for Julio to appear in that blank doorway.

Even had he been alone she would have offered a prayer of thanks, although it would have been hard to face the idea of Ramón being still in there and alone. Then suddenly the doorway was no longer empty and two of the firemen rushed forward when a tall, smoke-grimed figure appeared carrying another over his shoulder.

Dorcas closed her eyes briefly on the tears that ran unchecked down her cheeks and she found herself unable to move. Her legs seemed to have turned to water and refused to support her unless she clung to Doña Teresa, but Doña Teresa took only a second before she recovered, then she hurried over.

Close on her heels, Dorcas had no hesitation; she went straight to Julio and as he gently handed over his burden to the men, she hugged him close, heedless of the grime or of the stench of smoke about him, anxious only to assure herself that he was not hurt.

His body felt like fire through the thin shirt and he was still as tense as a coiled spring, but he put his arms around her tightly, his hands hard and urgent as he pressed her close to him, his face buried in the bright fairness of her hair. It seemed like hours that they stood like that, instead of the few moments it actually was, and an ambulance crew was already putting Ramón into the vehicle.

Doña Teresa turned and looked at them and there was a warm, gentle look of understanding in her dark eyes as she spoke. 'We owe you a great debt, Don Julio,' she said in her soft, quiet voice, then she looked at Dorcas. 'You will stay while I go with Ramón to the hospital, *niña*,' she told her. 'He is not hurt, thanks to Don Julio, and I know you would prefer to remain, *verdad*?'

'I would,' Dorcas agreed in a whisper, and looked up at the dark, smoke-grimed face that she had feared she would not see again. 'I'll stay,' she said, and didn't care if the fire crew or anyone else saw the smile she gave Julio or the bright glow in her eyes as she looked up at him.

The last vestige of sound dwindled away in the distance as the fire engines returned to San Julio, and the patio was silent once more. Its scents only briefly overcome by the stench of smoke, there were few traces of the fire to be seen from outside the house, and things might almost have been normal but for the state of Julio's once smart riding clothes and the smoke-blackened texture of his skin.

They had watched the fire engines depart in silence and now stood by the fountain in the cool peace of the night, looking at the broken window and the gaping black hole that had once been Ramón's bedroom. 'I was so afraid,' Dorcas whispered, half to herself, and shivered.

Julio's arm about her shoulders tightened its hold and he pulled her round to face him, lifting her chin with one grimy finger and looking down at her for a moment in silence. Being close to him like that, with the golden darkness of his body exposed by his torn shirt, and damp with his efforts to rescue Ramón, she felt suddenly and incredibly alive.

There was no sense of anti-climax, now that it was all over, she felt rather as if something much more important was only just beginning and her whole being shivered with strange new desires. One hand pressed the small of her back, until she was aware of every straining muscle in that steely body, and of the wild, erratic beating of her heart as she looked up at him, persuaded by that firm hand under her chin.

'You would have persuaded me not to go in there,' he said softly, and released her chin and put both arms round her. 'You knew of my fear, *amante*, did you not?'

Dorcas nodded while her fingers traced the out-

184

line of that dreadful reminder of the last time he had faced fire to effect a rescue. She looked up at him, her eyes searching the dark face with its glittering eyes and wide straight mouth, and that pale scar just below his jaw. A strong, hawkish face that she loved more than anything in the world. 'I know what it must have cost you to go in there for Ramón,' she said softly, 'and I'll never be able to thank you enough!'

Surprisingly he was smiling, that rakish, heart-stopping smile that could play such havoc with her senses, and he looked down at her with a deep glow in his dark eyes. 'You can, *enamorada*,' he said quietly. 'You can thank me in such a way that the debt, if there is one, will be paid a hundred times over!'

'Julio——' She looked up at him, and her heart was thudding so hard at her ribs that she could scarcely breathe for it. 'I don't know if——'

'*Mi amar!*' His hands drew her closer still and the warm, strong firmness of his body enveloped her with its tangy scents, made more pungent by the black smoke that streaked his face and arms as well as the golden smoothness of his chest.

He bent his head until the glittering black eyes filled her vision, and his mouth touched hers in a light, tentative kiss that parted her lips and brought a soft cry of pleasure from her as she slid her arms up to encircle his neck, her fingers curled in his thick dark hair.

'*Mi poco pichón!*' His kiss forced her head back and seemed to draw the last breath from her as she yielded to instincts both strange and exciting that would no longer be denied. 'My love, my sweet love!' He murmured the words against her ear, his face buried against the softness of her neck, his voice muffled by her hair, and he kissed the soft, smoothness of her throat and shoulders with a fervour that made her head spin.

'You will marry me?' he said in a deep, husky voice when he raised his head at last, and Dorcas smiled, her eyes bright and almost as dark as his in the moonlight.

'To repay the debt?' she asked softly, though she knew the answer well enough.

'And because I have loved you for so long, *mi enamorada*,' he told her, and kissed her again so fervently that she had little breath left to murmur anything more than a few words.

'I've never paid a debt more willingly,' she whispered.

THE OMNIBUS
Has Arrived!

A GREAT NEW IDEA
From HARLEQUIN

OMNIBUS

The 3-in-1 HARLEQUIN — only $1.95 per volume

Here is a great new exciting idea from Harlequin.
THREE GREAT ROMANCES — complete and
unabridged — BY THE SAME AUTHOR — in one
deluxe paperback volume — for the unbelievably
low price of only $1.95 per volume.

We have chosen some of the finest works of
world-famous authors and reprinted them in the
3-in-1 Omnibus. Almost 600 pages of pure entertainment for just $1.95. A TRULY "JUMBO" READ!

The following pages list some of the exciting
novels in this series.

Climb aboard the Harlequin Omnibus now! The
coupon below is provided for your convenience in
ordering.

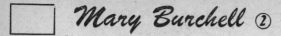

Mary Burchell ②

Omnibus

Mary Burchell has long been acclaimed "a writer to touch your heart." Her well-deserved fame can be attributed to the skillful blend of deep emotion, excitement, and happiness that she weaves into each one of her moving stories. Here we have chosen three of her most endearing novels.

. . . . CONTAINING

TAKE ME WITH YOU . . . the Dagram home was a warm and wonderful place. Leonie was so happy there, until that terrible night Lucas finally told her the truth. In desperation, she returned to the orphanage seeking comfort, only to find what both of them needed — the key that would set Lucas free . . . (#956).

THE HEART CANNOT FORGET . . . Antonia's cousin, Giles, should by all rights have inherited Deepdene Estate; but for some mysterious reason, he had been cast out. Slowly uncovering fragments of the family's history, Antonia began to understand the mystery, but everything she learned was directly linked with the woman Giles planned to marry . . . (#1003).

CHOOSE WHICH YOU WILL . . . Fourways was a rambling old house near Barndale, Middleshire. In this isolated English house, Harriet Denby became companion to Sophia Mayhew. Thus began the most confusing, tormenting experience of her young life, involving deceit, blackmail, and the disappearance of two people . . . (#1029).

only $1.95

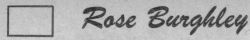

Rose Burghley

Omnibus

Through the years, devoted readers have become familiar with Rose Burghley's inimitable style of writing. And in the best tradition of the romantic novel, all her delightfully appealing stories have captured the very essence of romantic love.

. . . . CONTAINING

MAN OF DESTINY . . . Caroline was a compassionate and loving governess, whose only thoughts concerned the happiness of the neglected little boy in her care. But in the eyes of Vasco Duarte de Capuchos, Caroline's affectionate manner, and indeed Caroline herself, were far removed from his idea of a governess, and of a woman . . . (#960).

THE SWEET SURRENDER . . . the local Welsh folk knew it as Llanlyst, Castle of the Watching Eyes. When Paul Hilliard agreed to accompany her employer to this completely isolated castle on the coast, she had certain misgivings. The unexplained events that followed convinced her she had made a serious mistake . . . (#1023).

THE BAY OF MOONLIGHT . . . Sarah Cunninghame was a very attractive and graceful young woman. Philip Saratola was a distinguished, handsome man. But from the very beginning, their "accidental" relationship was bedevilled by misunderstandings. And the aggressive young Frank Ironside was determined that there would never be a relationship of any kind between them . . . (#1245).

only $1.95

Iris Danbury

Omnibus

Iris Danbury's popular and widely read novels have earned her a place high on the list of everyone's favorites. Her vital characterizations and choice of splendid locations have combined to create truly first class stories of romance.

. . . . CONTAINING

RENDEZVOUS IN LISBON . . . Janice Bowen entered Mr. Everard Whitney's office to inform him she no longer wished to work for him. When she left, her head reeled from the thought of accompanying him on a business trip to Lisbon. This was the first of many times that this impossible man was to astonish her . . . (#1178).

DOCTOR AT VILLA RONDA . . . Nicola usually ignored her sister's wild suggestions, but this one had come at the perfect time. Lisa had asked Nicola to join her in Barcelona. A few days after receiving the letter, Nicola arrived in Spain to discover that her sister had mysteriously disappeared — six weeks before she had written . . . (#1257).

HOTEL BELVEDERE . . . the fact that Andrea's aunt was head housekeeper at the large luxury hotel was sure to create ill feeling among her fellow employees. Soon after Andrea began work, their dangerous jealousy caused untold complications in Andrea's life — and in that of the hotel's most attractive guest . . . (#1331).

only $1.95

Amanda Doyle

Omnibus

To conceive delightful tales and to master the art of conveying them to literally thousands of readers are the keys to success in the world of fiction. Amanda Doyle is indeed a master, for each one of her outstanding novels is considered truly a work of art.

. . . . CONTAINING

A CHANGE FOR CLANCY . . . Clancy Minnow and her manager, Johnny Raustmann, were very happy running the Brenda Downs ranch in Australia. When the trustees appointed a new manager, Clancy had to break the news to Johnny. But Johnny Raustmann had a way out of this — for both of them . . . (#1085).

PLAY THE TUNE SOFTLY . . . when Ginny read the advertisement, it was the answer to both her prayers and her much needed independence. Immediately, she applied to the agency and was soon on her way to Noosa Homestead. But her brief happiness was shattered when she found that her new employer was none other than Jas Lawrence . . . (#1116).

A MIST IN GLEN TORRAN . . . after two years in Paris, Verona finally recovered from the death of her fiancé, Alex Mackinnon. When she returned to her Highland home, there were many changes at Glen Torran. But she discovered that Alex's younger brother, Ewan, still felt the estates he would inherit included Verona . . . (#1308).

only $1.95